Rebel Heart

Book Two of the Immortal Kindred Series

A.D. Brazeau

Rebel Heart
Book Two of the Immortal Kindred Series
Copyright © 2018 A.D. Brazeau
All rights reserved.

ISBN: (ebook) 978-1-945910-96-8
Print: 978-1-953335-51-7

Inkspell Publishing
207 Moonglow Circle #101
Murrells Inlet, SC 29576

Edited By Audrey Bobak
Cover art By Maria Spada

DEDICATION

For all those who possess their own rebel heart. Never give
up. The world needs you.

CHAPTER ONE

Annie

The ground was freezing, slick with mud. My hands, tied to a pole behind my back, tingled with lack of circulation. I knew I was in a tent. It was so dark when I came to, I couldn't see anything, but I could hear the flapping of the canvas walls in the gentle breeze.

Cold water dripped onto my shoulder from above. My head throbbed where someone had hit me from behind. A trickle of liquid oozed its way down my forehead, past my temple. Logic would tell me I've been captured by the English or the even more hated Hessians. Attempting to still my breathing, I concentrated on listening. Outside, I heard muffled voices, along with feet slapping in and pulling out of the muck with a sucking sound.

This was my sixth assignment as a Culper Spy. It had gone horribly wrong. Something stuck, pinched in my gut, from the moment I accepted this simple assignment. Deliver a message, this was all I had to do.

Handing off the missive to a shifty, wound-up man, I suppose the walls couldn't help but fall. With my head pounding and fuzzy, it was hard to remember everything. One thing I knew for sure was it hadn't felt right from the start. "You should learn to listen to yourself more, Annie. Now look what's happened," I mumbled to myself, trying to work my sleeping hands behind me.

I caught a clear word from a male voice just outside the tent. "Oh no, German," I thought to myself. This meant one thing, I had to get the hell out of these bonds now.

The English, depending on whose command they were under, would most likely treat me with unkindness. In a Hessian camp, however, there was no doubt I was in for the worst night of my life.

I started working the thick cord binding my wrists, hoping maybe I could slip my small hands out of the loosened loops. But they were so tight all I received for my efforts was torn skin. As painful as it was, the blood seeping from the cuts on my wrists allowed me to start freeing myself from the rope.

Just as I felt some hope beginning to light up inside me, the flap of the tent was pulled back. A very young soldier stood in front of me, holding up a lantern. A sour smell emanated from the man, no more than a boy. It was all I could do to keep my stomach from heaving. He smiled an almost toothless smile, prodding my leg with the toe of his boot, blathering on about something I could not understand. I assumed he was taunting me in an inappropriate way.

"I'll kill you if you touch me." I wasn't sure how I would make good on this threat, but it had to be said. He laughed in a gross, snorty way.

As this disgusting lecher started leaning down toward me, I began to gather spit in my mouth. Before I could let loose, another man strode into the tent. The officer yelled something in German at the profligate who came to attention, saluted, and left.

This man looked completely different from the other one. Not too young, tall, and muscular. His face was quite beautiful, with a full kissable mouth and sleepy blue eyes that could be sexy in a different circumstance. One thing I was grateful for was he didn't stink.

He wasn't smiling. He stood straight in front of me with hands clasped behind his back. His face was like stone, his mouth forming a perfect horizontal line. He regarded me, without speaking, for some time, as the terror in my heart grew. This was a man to be reckoned with. He may have been handsome, but he was a monster. I knew monsters when I saw them.

His Hessian's jacket was blue, trimmed in red. The distinctive Mitre Cap; an almost conical, golden hat, with a red tassel at the pointy top, towered on his head. There was no misidentifying a Hessian soldier when he wore this. I'd always thought the Mitre Cap was the most ridiculous, impractical-looking headgear a soldier could wear.

I thought at this moment what a fool I was. As much as I believed in this fight for independence, I simply did not have the physical strength to get through a situation like this. I closed my eyes for a moment, trying to accept my looming demise.

A shuffling sound caused me to look up, and I flinched. The scary, handsome German was now moving toward me. He crouched down, pulling a knife from his belt with a clang of metal against metal. I willed myself not to cry, not to scream, refusing to give them the satisfaction.

I'd known what I was getting into. This life was my choice, and the consequences were acknowledged, accepted without reservation. I believed in freeing the colonies from the English with everything I was.

Bracing myself, I gritted my teeth. Expecting pain at any moment, I instead felt the sweet release of my bonds being severed. I slouched forward, massaging and stretching out my arms. My mind reeled with various painful scenarios. What could this man have in store for me? My heart hammered away in my chest. Each beat felt dangerous, as if it could give out at any moment.

"Stand up now." The German's voice was deep but quiet. "Stand up now," he repeated after I failed to comply.

I tried to stand but was so sore I found it difficult to get my feet underneath me. An annoyed sigh escaped from my captor's lips. Instead of giving me time to stand, he grabbed my arms right below my shoulders, hauling me to my feet.

"Ouch," I exclaimed under my breath. The exclamation was involuntary, but I immediately regretted it. I sucked in air, planting my feet, with the expectation of a coming blow. The blow never came.

"Ouch," he said. "I don't know this word. If 'ouch' is an expression of pain, you can be rest assured, I am saving you from much more ouch than you can possibly imagine."

"What do you mean?" I asked as I continued to massage my arms.

"I'm taking you out of this camp, sending you on your way." He said all this without a speck of emotion in his voice or on his face.

My brows came together as I considered what he was saying. "Why? Why help me? I don't understand."

"It's simple. I don't believe in the interrogation of women."

"Thank you," I breathed it out as relief flooded my senses. Although, I couldn't quite believe his words. Was this a trick? Perhaps they meant to shoot me in the back as I fled. Surely, they were toying with me.

The German looked down at me, with what I would call disgust, a slight sneer marring his attractive face. "Don't thank me yet. We still must get out and I am by no means a hero, lady spy. I am a creature through and through. But this is a line not even I can cross."

"I understand. Thank you all the same." But I didn't understand, not at all. I stood there, trying to puzzle him out. For the life of me, I couldn't get a read on him.

"You will wait here until I return. When I come back, we will go. Our time will be limited." Turning, he began to walk away.

I was terrified for him to leave me but had no choice. Did this mean I was beginning to believe him? I must trust in his plan. Just before he reached the tent flap, I asked, "What's your name?"

"Captain Thayer Emmerich," he whispered over his shoulder and was gone.

My heart continued thumping out of my chest. If I didn't calm down, it wouldn't matter if the strange, beautiful German could spirit me out of this camp or not. My eyes were blurry from the pain in my head. What I really needed to do was lie down. It would likely be a while before I would be able to make myself comfortable.

"Breathe, Annie. Just breathe," I whispered to myself. I closed my eyes, willing my heart into a normal rhythm. I didn't know why I trusted this man, but I did. In the five minutes he was in front of me, I was astounded by the physical strength he exuded. Even though his grip on my arms was painful, I could tell he was restraining himself. I had the sense that if he had chosen to, he could've snapped my bones in half, as if they were kindling. What I wouldn't give to have strength like that. Physical strength of such magnitude would keep me from ever finding myself in another situation like this one.

After what seemed like an eternity, Thayer Emmerich returned.

"Put this on, now." He threw a ball of clothing at me. Unwinding it, I found a Hessian uniform.

"I can't wear this," I said, holding it toward him.

"Little girl, do you think you will be able to stroll out of this camp as you are? We will be spotted before we walk five feet. Spies should know about disguises. Put it on."

The "little girl" comment made me angry. I was a full-grown woman who up until today had been capable as a spy, but he was right. What I wore didn't matter. All that mattered was escaping this dreadful camp. I looked around for someplace to change.

"I'll turn around. Our window is closing, be quick."

"You'll have to unlace me first." I turned my back on him. I could have unlaced myself, but this would take time we didn't have. Captain Emmerich unlaced the back of my torn, muddy, black muslin gown. He was so quick, I couldn't register where his fingers were. Before I knew it, he'd finished. Could he really have unlaced me so fast, or was I just rattled? He turned back around.

I tossed the uniform on the dirty ground and began to shimmy out of my dress, which I kicked into the corner of the tent. Next came my chemise, which was also kicked aside. I was not unfamiliar with male garments. However, I was known for taking them off a man, not putting them on myself. The breeches, then the shirt confounded me.

After a bit of fumbling, the captain said, "Enough modesty," and turned around to help me into the uniform. I watched his face while he assisted me with the shirt. It remained completely blank. My voluptuous figure usually garnered quite the reaction from the opposite sex. This man was as cold and unmoving as a stone statue. I felt a small pang of disappointment, even if he was a Hessian.

"Follow behind me. Keep your head down and say nothing." He pointed to the ground for emphasis, as if I couldn't have comprehended what he meant.

I nodded my understanding and before I knew it, we were standing outside in the muck. Captain Emmerich took one brisk look to each side, then walked with an air of confident command toward the edge of the camp. It was dark with only a few lanterns lit and very few people about. This helped ease my anxiety. I tried walking with the same confidence, which was more difficult with my head down. The absurd cap threatened to fall off any minute, which would send a cascade of auburn curls falling around my shoulders.

Just as we were nearing the tree line, and I was beginning to relax, a soldier came running around the corner of a tent, right into the captain. The soldier snapped to attention, saluting. Captain Emmerich did the same, saying something in German. The young man relaxed, moving away.

As he walked by me, he looked me dead in the face, stopping in his tracks. I immediately put my head back down, but it was too late. It was obvious I was a woman in a man's uniform. There was no hiding this fact. The young man looked back at Captain Emmerich, turning as if he was about to run. The captain grabbed him by the neck with one hand. A sickening crunch reached my ears, right before the man crumpled into the mud.

"That was unfortunate," was all he said. The coldness of his voice shook me more than what he had just done.

I tried to hide my shock but knew I wasn't succeeding. "Why are you doing this for me? To kill your own man, it doesn't make sense," I said, still staring down at the young soldier.

"I'm beginning to wonder," he said as he grabbed my arm, yanking me into the dark woods. The trees looked ominous, and I hesitated just for a moment. Captain Emmerich took a handful of my uniform, at my shoulder this time, hauling me stumbling alongside him.

"Would you rather stay here? Would you like me to tell you all of the ugly things that will happen to you?" he said, striding with determination over tree roots and pine cones. The sharp, woodsy smell of the forest was welcome after the acrid scents of the camp.

I fell in line as we continued walking through the fragrant pine trees of New York. The night was pitch black as the moon was hidden behind thick cloud cover. I couldn't see my hands in front of my face. I felt as if in a tunnel, my senses strangely dulled by my blindness. Almost as soon as we set out, I fell on my knees after tripping over something hard, no doubt a large rock. Making our way through these woods seemed an impossible task.

"Captain Emmerich," I whisper-yelled.

"I'm here." I felt a steadying arm under my elbow helping me to my feet. Strange, he was almost tender.

"How can you see?" I asked. It was impossible. No one

would be able to see out here.

"I have excellent vision. I will guide you." The captain looped an arm around my waist, bringing me into his firm body.

Sharp vision didn't seem like an adequate explanation. My mind went back to the young man whose neck was crushed with more speed and force than should've been possible. I expected to feel warmth from his body, instead he felt cold through the uniform. Something was strange about this man. He was unusually attractive, strong, fast, and he could see in the dark without any problem. I couldn't help but laugh at myself.

"What's so funny?" he asked, irritation in his voice. "This doesn't seem like a humorous situation to me."

"It isn't. I'm more scared than I've ever been in my life."

"And yet you're laughing. Are you possibly mad?" he asked, in all seriousness.

"No, thank you. I'm not." I paused. "I believe the events of the night are causing me to think strange things. That's all."

"What sort of strange things are you thinking?"

"Well, it just occurred to me that you are unlike any man I've ever known." At this point, I wasn't so much walking as being carried.

"In what way?"

"Your strength and quickness, for one. Also, how can you possibly see right now? It doesn't make sense." My vision was also excellent, and I couldn't see my hand in front of my face.

"It makes perfect sense. You are correct, you are not thinking with clarity after the ordeal you have been through." The captain spoke in an even voice, and there was no evidence he was winded by all his effort.

"Maybe. I assume you're going back to your camp. How will the dead soldier be explained? And how did I come to be there? Events are fuzzy," I said, exploring the back of my head with my fingers.

"Strange things happen out in the woods. My men will accept whatever vague explanation I give them. They do not question me or my command. As to how you came to be here, you were handed over by someone who wants a favor from the English. Who it was, I can't say. I wasn't there for the exchange."

I didn't like what he said one bit. Someone in the network betrayed me? It didn't seem possible. Or, maybe I just didn't want it to be possible. But it had been known to happen. We either had a turncoat or a mole. I was sure it was the man I handed the message to. I would have to discuss this with my handler, Benjamin, when I saw him next.

"Wouldn't they then obey your command to let me go?" I asked as I continued stumbling over every branch and stone in my way. He seemed to be contradicting himself.

"Another was coming in to interrogate you. Someone who outranks me." His voice became clipped. This night was one of the strangest I had passed.

"What will you say happened to me?"

"I will say you escaped, that I was searching the woods for you. Enough talk for now." It was clear he no longer wished to discuss any of this, but my questions were far from answered.

The sounds in the darkness were few; our feet crunching the forest floor, crickets chirping, and the occasional ominous hoot of an owl. The night was so dark and cold, the walk so long, I thought I was hallucinating when I began to see a small light in the distance. It wasn't until I smelled the smoke from a chimney that I realized it must be a cabin. My limbs were shaking with weariness, and I hoped I would finally be able to rest. A warm fire also sounded heavenly.

"What is that?" I asked.

"That is where I leave you," he said quietly, relaxing his grip on my waist.

I was beginning to feel so comfortable with this odd man. I could feel the fear rising again at the thought of being left alone.

"You're leaving me?" Not meaning to, I clutched at his hand, hating myself for the weakness.

Captain Emmerich extricated his hand from mine. "Yes, you will be fine. This is the home of an old man and his wife. They do things for me on occasion."

"Things?" I asked, thinking this man could not be any stranger.

"Yes, things," he said, cutting off any more questions I may have.

This powerful German was a deep, mysterious puzzle I very much wanted to unravel. By the time we reached the door of the small log cabin, I could feel the blood from my ravaged feet pooling in my borrowed, ill-fitting boots. The captain knocked only once, loud and clear. Seconds later, the door was opened by a small, bent man with wisps of white hair sprouting from the top of his head. He wore only a nightshirt.

Captain Emmerich said something in German. The man nodded as the captain pushed me inside.

"They will give you a dress and see you back to the city."

I could see his face again, from the glowing fire inside the tiny home. "That's it?" I asked him, my eyes searching his.

"What else would there be?" His features remained as cold as ever.

I sighed and said, "Thank you for what you did for me. Will I ever see you again?"

For just one second, I thought I saw a flicker of some unidentifiable emotion darken his eyes. "Unlikely."

He turned and was swallowed up by the blackness of the night.

CHAPTER TWO

Annie

Waking up in a bed felt like a dream. Snuggling deeper into the warm mattress, I tried not to think about the pain in my body. All I wanted to do was revel in the warmth of the blankets, and the pleasant smell from the rosewater I splashed over my skin before losing myself to sleep.

My wrists and arms were still sore from my bonds, the skin pulsing with each beat of my heart. My torn, blistered feet were also throbbing in their bandages. But, I was safe and alive. The gratitude I felt for Captain Emmerich knew no bounds. I would never be able to thank him enough for what he did to get me out of his camp. I hoped he would not be punished for it by his superiors.

What an eccentric man; almost otherworldly. He didn't seem to belong among the rest of us. Those sleepy eyes set in such a beautiful face would haunt me, I was sure of it. His near tenderness as I fell in the woods had made my stomach flop in a pleasant way. He didn't smell like the rest of his camp. Instead, he smelled of the forest, like pine trees and leaves. His scent had calmed me, helped me to feel more grounded.

I propped myself up on my elbows, looking around the small room. It was plain with solid, shaker furnishings, but this inn's little room was like a palace compared to the wet tent and the musty, dirty cabin in the woods.

The captain was right when he said the elderly couple would see me safely the rest of the way. The old woman, almost an exact copy of her husband, gave me a decent enough gown of cream-colored muslin, brown boots, which fit, and a brown cloak. The items were even clean, something I had not expected.

I had peered into the small room from which the woman produced the dress. It was stocked with all manner of items, not likely seen in so poor a cabin. It appeared they were meant to be prepared for whatever the mysterious captain asked of them.

After I dressed, the old man brought around two saddled, shabby horses to the front of the meager home. There would be no resting. He held the reins of one horse toward me. I took them and mounted, worrying about the frail animal beneath me.

The old woman, never having said a word, closed the door and was gone. Her husband mounted his own horse with the agility of a much younger man, springing into the saddle with a lightness which seemed unnatural. He clucked his tongue, spurring the horses forward. The sky was lightening, so I could at last see my surroundings. There wasn't much to this place but a small, leaning structure behind the cabin; the dilapidated home of the horses we now rode. Pine trees and wilderness surrounded us. The morning birds merrily chirped overhead, the only cheerful element to a rather dismal scene.

We rode for hours in silence, until coming upon an English checkpoint, outside of the city. I reined in my horse, stopping us dead in our tracks. My chest constricted in fear. The old man looked back at me and beckoned me forward. I had no choice but to trust he knew what he was doing. It was doubtful Captain Emmerich would go to this much trouble without a plan to see me all the way through. I had trusted him this far.

Reaching the English soldiers, the old man pulled out a paper from inside his pocket and placed it in the waiting hand of the tired-looking Redcoat. The soldier nodded, handed the paper back to my elderly escort, and we were once again on our way. Was this all due to luck or something else? Exhausted to the point of illness, I didn't much care. I suspected the captain, like most of us in this war, had his own secret dealings.

Shortly thereafter we stopped. The old man dismounted, taking the reins of my horse as I placed my feet on the ground with care.

He pointed down the road, but I already knew the way from here.

"Thank you," I said, unsure if he would understand me. I had said this a lot in the last few hours.

He nodded and remounted his horse, leaving me alone to make my way back to the inn I was temporarily calling home. I hobbled the best I could on ruined feet.

Being that I was still in English-occupied territory, I was forced to continue to dissemble. My cover was one of a farmer's daughter with forged papers, which allowed me in and out of the city. The papers stated my position as a go-between for my father and the food merchants in New York. A pretty smile, sparkling brown eyes, and heaving bosom didn't hurt either.

I was to meet my handler, Benjamin, at The Red Lion for breakfast. He was in New York to supervise my pursuits, as well as other Culper Spies whose identities I did not know. Last evening upon returning, I sent him a note in our code, my hands shaking. I let him know I had been in trouble and wanted to get out of the city for a while.

Needing to keep under the radar, I dressed in a simple navy-blue gown with a creamy lace fichu draped around my neck and tucked in over my bosom. I pulled on elbow-length gloves, even though it was unseasonably warm, to cover the contusions and cuts on my wrists. The bruises, now dark purple, on my upper arms were naturally covered by the sleeves of my gown. Thank goodness for the modesty of women's clothing.

Wincing, I slid my blistered feet into the most comfortable slippers I owned. Walking today would not be easy, but there was nothing to be done about it. Relaxing in bed was not a luxury I could partake in. I covered my pinned-up hair with a lace cream cap. No jewelry would be worn, save the gold wedding band on my left hand. The band was a wonderful deterrent. The morning preparation gave me time to think about Captain Emmerich.

I hadn't known many Hessians, but the stories I'd heard about them were not for the faint of heart. They were no better than hired thugs, doing the English's dirty work. I was still in shock the captain chose to show me mercy. Not only did he help, but he took out one of his own men to save me. His behavior was certainly incongruous to what I knew about Hessians.

I thought of how attractive he was. His uniform had a hard time hiding a muscular and well-defined body. As he held me to him in the forest, I could feel his well-developed bicep pressed into my back. There was another power, one he seemed to emanate from within. I was sure it was my terror. Exhaustion, too, had overtaken me, but something about him hadn't seemed quite human. Those eyes were entrancing, languid and sexy. Too bad I'd likely never see him again. I shrugged my shoulders, ready to get on with my responsibilities.

The spring day was warming up and would prove nice. I wouldn't require a cloak, so I threw on a light knit shawl. Leaving my sparse, but safe boarding room to walk onto the streets of New York seemed a little daunting after what I had been through. I squared my shoulders, screwed up my courage, and made myself ready to meet Benjamin. Seeing my friend was worth any discomfort.

The street was already bustling as I stepped out to join the world, trying my best not to limp. An early robin pranced his way down the side of the road. Ladies and gentlemen were on their way to engage in some business or other. The laughter of children, on their way to the school one block over, brought a smile to my face. Horses, attached to rumbling carts, made their way up and down the streets with no one to clean up after them.

The roads were a little muddy from the season's rains, so there was an earthy smell in the air mixed with the scents of horses and bodies. I thought how lovely it must be to live in the country, surrounded by flowers, trees, and sweet fresh smells. City life seemed all I was meant for.

I arrived at the meeting house before Benjamin, floorboards creaking with each step. I secured a corner table in the dark, rather empty pub. Two coffees along with a couple of sweet rolls were ordered, then I scanned the room. Other than the proprietor, it was just me and two elderly, life-weary men. They sat playing chess against the back wall, paying me no mind; the heavy, wooden furniture concealing me from prying eyes.

I didn't have to wait long before my friend strode through the door. Benjamin Tallmadge was a tall, trim man with dark hair and well-defined features. He dressed impeccably, always a gentleman. As soon as he saw me, his face lit up with a bright, gentle smile. Our food and coffee arrived just as he sat opposite me. Once our host left, Benjamin reached across the table, grasping my hand.

"Tell me what happened. Your note indicated you were in danger." Benjamin spoke in the low tones of someone telling a secret, but no one was listening.

"I'm safe now. I was double-crossed making the drop yesterday and taken prisoner by a troop of Hessians," I said, pausing to give him a moment to respond.

Benjamin's face was aghast. He squeezed his eyes shut, not letting go of my hand for a second and said, "Annie, my

God. Do you know who betrayed you? How did you escape? Did they hurt you?" He spat out his questions, one after the next.

"I wasn't hurt. The only wounds I incurred were some bruises and cuts from the ropes. I've an idea the snake was the man I handed off the message to, Thomas, but since I was hit over the head, I can't really be sure what happened. I was released by the captain."

"I'll deal with Thomas, but released?" Benjamin's eyes were now wide with disbelief.

"Yes, actually it was more than a release. He helped me escape." I recounted the night's events for Benjamin as he stared at me with a gaping mouth.

"This is unbelievable. Why would he help you? I'm so grateful he did, I just don't understand why. Even for you, with your charms, this seems impossible." Benjamin rubbed at his eyes with his free hand.

"He said he doesn't believe in the interrogation of women, but that was all. He had to make it look like an escape, so he wouldn't be in trouble with his superior officer, whoever that is." I picked up the coffee cup, gulping the precious liquid without grace.

"Annie, you are lucky. So very lucky. You cannot expect anything like this to happen again. The next time you are captured, it will be your last. I wish you would reconsider your involvement. There are other ways to help the cause."

"I know. I've been thinking about this, believe me. I was terrified last night, more so than I've ever been in my life. I kept thinking of all the things they could do to me. I'm exhausted, scared, and sore. But I need to go on. I must get right back out there. We are making such progress, Benjamin. We're close to winning, I know it. This fight, there is nothing more important. I've been a good asset so far. Please don't shut me out. I want to continue. This is my choice."

Benjamin squeezed my hand, lowering his head. "All right, Annie. When have I ever won an argument against you? If only we all had your fire. This revolution would've been over a long time ago if we had a hundred more like you. I have something quick and easy for you to do, tonight. Then, tomorrow you are to go back to Boston to await further orders. You may not like it, but you do need a bit of rest after this trial, and that's an order, soldier."

I agreed, not admitting out loud how getting out of English-occupied New York and being home for a while sounded wonderful.

"What is the mission?" I asked, picking at the sweet bun.

"A simple one. I have a message, which I will pass you under the table." He paused, moved his hand to his pocket, and then under cover toward me. I gripped the piece of paper, slipping it into my own pocket. The last mission was supposed to be simple, as well. Instead, I found myself tied up in the enemy's camp.

"You will take this to All Soul's Cemetery. Near the back of the graveyard is a grave with the name of Earl Golden. Set into the gravestone is a symbol, an hourglass with wings. Pull the hourglass out toward you, slip the message behind, and then replace it. That is all. I suggest you go right before nightfall. In the morning, head straight back to Boston. Do you still have your papers?"

"Yes, everything is ready. An hourglass with wings? What does it mean?" I knew enough by now to know everything had a meaning. I also knew the simple task was something Benjamin could easily have done himself. He was giving me this assignment to help me feel more settled after what happened.

"It symbolizes the swiftness with which time passes. For us, this means the time of the rebellion is rapidly coming to an end."

"Yes, it is. I feel it, Benjamin. We are close," I said, feeling all the uncertainty would be worth it when this was over.

"Many of us feel this way, Annie. I can't thank you enough for all you have done for the cause. It hasn't always been easy. Seducing Major Fortenberry must have been most repugnant. You have taken on each challenge with a fearlessness that is admirable. Most men could not have made the sacrifices you have."

"Thank you, Benjamin. The major was not my favorite job, but the information I was able to pass on to you was worth every second. I regret nothing. Don't forget everything I've done has been my choice. I could have said no to anything, anytime. I'm proud of what I've done for the cause." I paused, thinking about last night. "I only wish I possessed the physical strength of a man. If I were stronger, I would've been more able to fight my captors, perhaps getting away before they were able to get me to their camp."

"Unfortunately, we can't do anything about that. But, I do have something for you, something I should have given you long before now which will be of use."

"Benjamin, if it's a weapon…"

Benjamin held up his hand, interrupting me, "I know how you feel already. They are cumbersome, difficult to conceal. It's important to me you have the means with which to defend yourself. I promise it is small and light. Here…"

Once again, he reached into his pocket and pulled out an object. I caught a momentary glimpse of a golden glint before he reached it underneath the table. My hand met his as he passed me what felt like cold metal. He was right, it was small, lightweight. I slipped this alongside the note. There would be time to look at it later.

"Tell me more about this captain from last night. Leave nothing out," said Benjamin, turning his attention to his coffee.

I recounted every detail for him. I even included the strange aspects about Captain Emmerich which had caught my attention. "He seemed so powerful in a way I can't quite describe. And he was fast. So fast, he made me feel as if I was hallucinating."

Benjamin didn't say anything for a moment. Then he rubbed his hands together and said, "You need to come back to my room with me. I have to show you something."

"Benjamin, after all this time," I joked, bringing the coffee cup to my lips. He shyly looked away and didn't laugh, although the corners of his mouth threatened to twitch upward.

We finished the rest of our meager morning meal, then rose together from the table. Benjamin took my hand, tucking it into the crook of his arm. Walking down the street with him would normally be something I enjoyed. As it was, I winced with every step, hoping we would soon reach our destination.

Once we arrived at his boarding house, he took me around the back, so we could sneak up the servants' stairs. His room was rather nice, much nicer than mine, I thought with a little rancor. He told me to close the door as he stooped to pull a plain wooden box out from under his bed. Benjamin fished a key from his pocket before fitting it into the lock.

I tried to take in everything inside the strange vessel. On the underside of the box lid was a diagram of a monster with fangs. Along the side was a recess filled with small bottles of clear liquid, each marked with a cross. The middle compartment contained whole bulbs of garlic, and the section on the other side held what looked like silver bullets. Benjamin pulled out a drawer on the bottom, revealing a revolver, a crucifix, and several pieces of pointed wood.

"Benjamin, what is this?" I ran my finger over the cold metal of the bullets.

"It's my slayer box," Benjamin said, with no trace of laughter.

"Your what?" I tried to keep the shock from my voice.

"Annie, I know how this must look to you. I don't have time to go into it all right now. To put it succinctly, vampires are attracted to wars."

"Vampires? Benjamin, stop. This is crazy." This was not

the first time I heard this superstition. But, legend was all it could be. A vampire was simply another mythical creature.

"You know I'm not crazy. Think about the man who helped you escape last night. You know there was something off about him. You said so yourself. All I want you to do, for now, is keep an open mind and carry these." Benjamin pulled out the crucifix, along with one of the bottles of liquid. "This is holy water. If you throw it on a vampire, it will burn their skin."

I refused to laugh at my friend. I knew he was as sane as I was. I'd known a lot of superstitious people, so I humored him and took the items.

I noticed a small leather book on the bedside table. "If that's the code book, you should probably do a better job of hiding it."

Benjamin's eyes widened, his cheeks blushing a deep crimson. He took the book and slipped it into his coat. "I was in a hurry. I never leave it out. How did you recognize it?"

I reached out to squeeze his arm. "Benjamin, I was making a jest. You must be more careful, my friend."

I left Benjamin with a promise to be on high alert and returned to my boarding room to pack my few belongings. I didn't look at the message he had given me. It wasn't for me and was in code anyway. Although, I could have broken it if I wished.

I pulled out the weapon he'd passed to me at the pub. It was a beautiful creation, an Ottoman dagger. The hilt was crafted in jade, carved with leaves and scalloped designs. The blade was copper with beautifully etched, looping scrolls. The sheath was also copper with the same intricate impressions. The dagger was sharp, yet light, small enough to fit in my pocket without being noticed. This was the key. I could not carry anything which could be detected, which was why I refused to carry the pistol Benjamin tried to give me when I first joined the network. I was grateful to have it. This knife would give me some peace of mind.

I slipped out of the inn with an hour to go until sunset. This would be my last mission for the time being. Although I didn't admit it, I was looking forward to the break.

Walking through the city to the cemetery was no easy task. By the time I reached the iron gates, my feet screaming with each step, it was close to dark. Thoughts of my warm, cozy home assailed my mind. What I wouldn't give to be there right now.

I shouldn't have come so late in the evening. I carried a small lantern, but the place was so deserted, so eerie, unease prickled the back of my neck. An evening mist hung about the gravestones like a death shroud. There were no sounds, only a smell of decay which made me shudder.

I tried to tell myself this was an easy task, but something still didn't feel right. Shaking my head clear of these thoughts, I pressed on.

I looked around just to be certain I was alone. The grave was right where Benjamin said it would be. His precise directions saved me much time. Walking through this desolate place brought back a myriad of unwanted memories.

As an eight-year-old child, I had seen both of my parents buried within weeks of each other. The influenza was dreadful, unforgiving. Being poor, they were buried cheaply, with no one in attendance but myself and the priest. The next day, I was picked up by my mother's cousin. The penniless woman was not happy to have another mouth to feed. But I was used to work and proved myself useful to her. Benjamin said I had been trying to prove my worth ever since.

I set down my lantern, then tugged at the winged hourglass. It took a bit of teasing but finally came loose. I slipped in the message, replacing the symbol without delay. Snatching up the lantern, I began to walk with haste back out of the graveyard. All I wanted to do was leave that dreary place with as much speed as I could muster on my injured feet.

In my mind, I was already at the inn, where I was warming up, eating a filling meal, and turning in early. My arms felt better, but it would be a week or so until my feet fully healed. Tomorrow morning, I would begin the two-day journey back home. Just as I was about to exit the cemetery gates, a familiar figure loomed before me.

CHAPTER THREE

Annie

"Captain Emmerich," I said as I almost jumped out of my skin.

"Good evening, Miss? It occurs to me I never asked for your name, or do you prefer not to give it?"

I didn't see what it would hurt for him to know my name. The man helped me escape, after all. However, his presence in this cemetery at the exact moment I dropped a message sent alarm bells ringing through my head.

"Annie Monroe. What are you doing here? Are you alone?" I asked, looking around.

"Yes, I'm alone, no need to fear." He paused, looking around himself. "What are you doing here?" he asked, turning the question around on me.

"Just visiting a friend," I answered, with the saddest eyes I could rally. I was pretty sure he knew the truth. It was no mere coincidence which brought the captain here tonight.

"Hm-hmm. By chance would your friend be Earl Golden?"

I kept my face blank, my breathing natural. I was practiced in deception, but there was still a pit of sour acid working in my stomach. "Are you spying on me, Captain?"

"Spying on the spy? Perhaps, I am. I hoped after last night, you would give this up, or at least stop for more than twenty-four hours. I think I'll just go and see what it is you've left behind." He started to move around me.

"No," I said, blocking his way with my body, tiny in comparison to his. He laughed, making my blood boil. I pulled out my newly acquired dagger, unsheathed it, and held it in front of me.

He stopped laughing, looking down at my knife without moving his head. "This is not a game, Annie Monroe. It is war and we are on opposing sides."

"Of course, this isn't a game. I'll die before I let you get to that gravestone. Are you ready to kill me, Captain?" I stood as tall as I could, which was still not nearly as tall as the man in front of me. "I am in this for the honor of my fellow countrymen, and you are nothing but a paid mercenary." This seemed to rankle him, as his shoulders visibly twitched.

"There is far more to my involvement than you might think. I have as personal a stake in the outcome of this as you."

"And what is that?" I didn't move a muscle.

"Certainly not something I can share with you." Captain Emmerich relaxed his stance, moving back two paces. "I don't wish to harm you, not after I went to such great lengths to save you. I suppose I can let one message go."

"You don't seem like someone who wholeheartedly believes in what they are doing," I observed, not backing down yet.

"I believe in my cause… It's you." Captain Emmerich's accent was strong, but he enunciated his words so beautifully there was no misunderstanding him. Although, I must have misunderstood him because I was baffled.

"Me?" was all I could respond with.

"Yes, you. You are infuriating. You're fire, bravery, and…"

"And?" I slipped the dagger back in its sheath, returning it to the recesses of my pocket. I did this to give myself something else to do with my eyes. I felt blotchy heat rise to my neck, spreading its way onto my face. A feeling of butterflies replaced the sourness in my stomach.

My physical reaction increased my nervousness. This was not something I usually felt with men I found attractive. They were almost always a means to an end for me. This man, however, was making me feel like an untouched bride on her wedding night; jittery and unsure.

"And, nothing." The captain paused, looking around once again. "I have always loved cemeteries. They are places of quiet contemplation. I have been contemplating many things in the last few hours, Miss Monroe. Specifically, why you have come into my life and why I should care so much about your welfare. I am not one to concern myself with others."

I wanted to say, "Of course, you don't. You work for the English, those who would oppress liberty and freedom." Instead, I said, "I came into your life by chance. There is no other reason. As for why you seem so interested in my safety, only you can answer such a question. And cemeteries are for reflection, but they are also settings of deep sadness, not places to be loved."

He looked at me, his face unreadable, as always.

"Have you been trained to hide your emotions?" I asked, genuinely interested. This was something I could use more practice with. Skilled as I was, I sometimes felt as if my face betrayed what I was thinking and feeling when it should always be a mask like his.

"No, I have acquired no training in what you ask. I am simply not accustomed to feeling." He said this so matter of fact, like feeling was not a natural state for a human being.

"That's unfortunate. There is so much to be felt in the world if you would only allow yourself."

"There is also much to lose in feeling. It is best to keep emotions in check, especially in my line of work. I wanted to pass on to you the name of the man who betrayed you. All my lieutenant could give me was a first name; Thomas." At this, he turned his back on me and started walking away.

So, Thomas was the one, and just as I thought. I would write down this confirmation and send it to Benjamin as soon as I was back in my room.

"Wait!" I cried, not intending to yell. "Will you walk me home? I've stayed much later than I intended. It's getting dark." I hoped he would say yes, less because I wanted the protection and more because he had piqued my curiosity.

The captain stopped, holding out his left arm for me to take. "Let us make haste, I have things to see to."

"I can't walk too fast. My feet are battered and blistered, and I appreciate the name. You didn't have to tell me."

He made a grunt which sounded like an acceptance. I stepped forward, taking his arm. "Thank you. The favors I owe you are piling up," I said, again.

Captain Emmerich didn't acknowledge this. We began to walk back toward the center of town in silence. After several minutes, I noticed the captain gazing down at my hand in a manner I would call sweet. His eyes had softened, a slight smile playing on his lips. We appeared as any couple; strolling down the lane, arm in arm.

This man was a walking conundrum. He was hard, powerful, and merciless toward his own men. With me he had shown nothing but kindness, saving me from certain death or worse. He then allowed a message from a revolutionary to remain in place and gave me the name of my betrayer. Something was still nagging at me, though.

"You were following me, weren't you? It was no coincidence that you were in the cemetery."

"Not following so much as watching." His face went hard again, eyes facing front.

"Watching?" Maybe I should be afraid of him, after all. How would he even know where to find me? "What do you mean, watching? Watching and following are synonymous." I stopped, pulling back on his arm.

"I was concerned about you. I wanted to make sure you made it safely back to the city without issue and give you the information I received. I had a man on you. It needn't be more complicated than that."

I wasn't sure what to think about this. This German was my enemy, although he had played the guardian angel. My first instinct told me he was toying with me, looking for information regarding my dealings. He was attractive, and perhaps his game was to seduce me, as I had seduced so many others. Perhaps, I was about to get a taste of my own medicine. If so, I was in danger, as were the people I worked with. Benjamin, in particular.

I decided to call him out. This was a risky move, but if I watched his face close enough, I may be able to catch him. "Are you manipulating me, Captain? Hoping to find something useful to use for the English?"

"I'm not a soldier, right now. Although, I should be. I am not doing my duty. Somehow, I am unconcerned with that for the time being. Truly, I only wanted to make sure you were safe, and remaining out of harm's way. I am disappointed as you still seem hell-bent on involving yourself in dangerous matters." He looked me in the eye as we stood in the road.

I should not like this man, as he represented everything I loathed. Still, there seemed to be so much more to him than meets the eye. I could not deny how powerfully attractive I found him. He still carried with him the scent of pine from the forest.

I noticed for the first time he was out of uniform, wearing the street clothes of every other middle-class man. His sudden appearance in the cemetery left me too startled to observe this detail. Without his enormous helmet covering his head, he had very thick, wavy hair which teased the tops of his ears. Something made me want to run my hands through the warmly brown mane. I checked myself.

"I'm not sure what to say, Captain Emmerich."

"Call me Thayer, Miss Monroe. And you don't have to

say anything. It's probably better if you don't. I will drop you at the inn, leave, and that will be the end of this. Nothing more can there be between us."

"You're right. Our positions are too impossible and different. And, you can call me Annie." I took his arm again as we continued our walk. The streets of the city were dark, save for an occasionally lit street lamp. It was quiet, too. The city blocks, lined with brick buildings and clapboard houses, should have been much busier with people on their way home or to the pub for the evening. Only once did a straggler pass us by.

Halfway back to the inn, Thayer's body stiffened. We came to a halt. He placed his right hand on top of mine, turning his body to put me more behind him, rather than beside him. He seemed alert, like an animal. What was he shielding me from? I stood on my tip toes, peeking over his shoulder; there was nothing. The night was still, and no one was about.

"What is it?" I whispered.

Thayer's profile reminded me of a lion who had spotted prey. His mouth was set in a hard line. His blue eyes scanned the street with the wildness of an animal. His body remained still as a statue, although his knees were slightly bent, as if he might pounce at any moment. Still, I could see nothing. There was no noise, save for the occasional, far-off bark of a dog.

"Move into the alley," was all he said, so low I almost didn't hear him.

"Why?"

He didn't wait for me to move of my own volition, instead he pushed me backward until we were both enveloped by the black darkness of the alleyway. My left hand moved instinctively to my pocket, feeling for my dagger. Almost as soon as we were under cover, I could feel Thayer's body relax.

"It was nothing. I thought I saw something out of the corner of my eye, in the shadow of the building across the street."

"What was it?" I asked, not convinced.

"I thought it was a person, watching us, but there is no one now. I'm sorry if I alarmed you," he said, still looking into the street.

"You did alarm me. Are you sure you didn't see anyone? Could it have been the person you sent to follow me?" My body was still tense.

"No, it was nothing. My senses are a little unnerved, is all. Let's get you safely to your destination."

He offered no further explanation. I continued to be on high alert; my hand inside my dress, holding my dagger, my eyes scanning every which way.

Without further incident, we reached the stoop in front of my temporary home. The lamp outside the door was unlit, leaving us in a cover of darkness. A darkness which spoke of clandestine meetings and star-crossed lovers.

I removed my hand from Thayer's arm, turning to face him. I felt conflicted by this parting. I would have loved the chance to get to know this mysterious man, but this was not the time to kindle a friendship, or anything else. A part of me wanted to ask him up to my meager, little room.

"Goodnight, Annie. Please take care of yourself," said Thayer, clasping his hands behind his back. The soldier, once again.

Unable to leave, I did a very impulsive thing; I stood on my tip toes, pulled him down to me by his shoulders, and planted a quick kiss on his lips. I stepped back, releasing him, about to add my goodbye to his. Instead, Thayer moved his arm around my waist, pulling me back up toward him. With his other hand, he brushed a loose curl from my cheek, cupping the back of my head, and pressed his lips, slowly and softly to mine. I didn't resist in any way. I melted into his arms, becoming clay for him to mold.

I pushed back against his warm mouth. My hands rested against the hardness of his chest. I didn't want to feel anything, but within moments, something unlocked inside me. The doorway hadn't fully opened, but it was cracked. No one had ever gotten so far, certainly not after one kiss. We stood outside the inn, locked in an embrace, kissing with a passion I had never felt before. Everything inside me wanted to invite him in. I was just about to throw caution to the wind, when he broke away, releasing me.

"I'm sorry. That was not appropriate." He took a step back, seeming unable to look me in the eyes.

"I'm not sorry. I know this is crazy, and we should hate each other. Instead, I feel drawn to you."

I reached for him and he grasped my hands, placing them back down at my sides. With his head down, he said, "I cannot allow myself to feel anything for you. Goodnight, Miss Monroe. I wish you all the best."

And just like that, he was gone. I was startled, confused. He left with such speed; no one could move so fast. One second, he was standing in front of me, the next, he was gone. My rational mind told me he should only be a few steps away. Instead, he was nowhere to be seen. I contributed my disorientation to the darkness, and the kiss, but the same odd feeling about him continued to nag at me. He was not like anyone else.

I reluctantly went inside. Back in my room, I removed my dress and slipped into bed. My feet were still throbbing. Something else didn't feel right; my heart. What was it about that man, besides the obvious? I'd known many handsome men in my twenty-eight years. Never had I known someone who had taken my breath away the way Thayer Emmerich just had. There was no way of getting in touch with him. The thought of never seeing him again was distressing. They said war made strange bedfellows. The statement was certainly true in my case.

Only Thayer would never be my bedfellow in the way I would like. I wondered if Benjamin would know how to find a Hessian captain. He would be furious if I told him about tonight and the possible compromise of the dropped message. I supposed the only thing to do was to get up tomorrow, go home, and stop thinking about the German with the blue bedroom eyes. If only it were so easy.

Thayer

Annie Monroe has no idea the danger she's in, I thought, as I left her in front of the small, dingy inn. The kiss was a mistake, and I was smart enough to know that. No matter if her lips had been remarkable. Angry with myself for losing control of my senses, I did the only logical thing I could think of. I disappeared. It was risky, leaving her in such a way. She must have wondered how I could leave so fast, but it didn't matter. I would never see her again. Her mind would make up whatever excuse it needed to explain the sudden departure.

I stood for some time in the darkness opposite the inn. I wasn't sure why I lingered. Maybe I was hoping to catch a glimpse of her body silhouetted behind the curtain of her room. Maybe I just wanted to make sure she was in for the night, safe from harm. Walking her home, I found myself jumping at shadows. Now I was sure it had been nothing. If Emilia were lurking somewhere near, she wouldn't hide it.

The thought of never again seeing those soft brown eyes gazing into mine filled me with an unfamiliar feeling. Was it sadness? Loss? These emotions were unknown to me. The only emotion I had a solid relationship with was anger. This feeling served me well as a vampire and now as a soldier, with a very specific assignment. Annie would do nothing but get in the way of this mission. I had a duty to my family. I would fulfill this duty and forget about the woman with the fiery passion.

I would face some trouble when Emilia Romanov found out I had let a possible Culper Spy leave camp, killing one of my men in the process. My excuse would have to be a creative one. Emilia Romanov was the most ruthless, unfeeling being I had ever known, vampire or otherwise.

Her only concern was the survival of the family. Nothing else ever entered her consciousness.

She would not care how I felt something stir inside of me as I looked upon Annie Monroe, bound and afraid inside a dirty, wet tent. She would not understand the feeling of protectiveness, along with something else I couldn't name at the time. Emilia Romanov wouldn't even care to try.

I was family, and this gave me some license. Some. She would punish me, then forget it, if I returned to acting as a good soldier should. This was the only time I ever failed her. But Annie, I could not get her out of my mind. The warmth of her soft, voluptuous body as I pulled her to me. The feeling of her sweet, heart-shaped mouth. The scent of roses making my head swim. She had done something to me, this was undeniable. I would simply have to forget her, push her from my mind.

Annie's world was dangerous enough without me in it. I would only expose her to something far more insidious, more terrifying than she could ever imagine. What Emilia would do to Annie would make the most hard-hearted, battle-weary warriors turn away in horror. I would serve Annie best by staying far away from her. Remaining in New York would be a death sentence, as vulnerable as she was.

Annie Monroe may have had the fiercest, most independent spirit I'd ever known anyone to have, mortal or immortal, but her frail human body was her weakness. A weakness she could never escape from.

I returned to camp with an hour to spare until sunrise. On the desk inside my lonely, uninviting tent sat a letter sealed with black wax and the mark of Emilia Romanov—a crow's foot. I sat in my straight-backed chair, taking a moment before breaking the seal.

Thayer, my son. I understand there was some confusion concerning your escapee. Because of this, I have delayed my arrival. You know what we seek. I expect you to acquire the item by the time I arrive. Emilia

I crumpled the note, tossing the ball of paper on the desk, and slumped back in the chair. All I could hope for was Annie would stay out of harm's way.

A.D. BRAZEAU

CHAPTER FOUR

Annie

The man claimed me with a kiss. I woke with my still sore body, ready to leave New York. My spirit, however, wanted to remain on the chance I would see Thayer, once again. This was foolishness. Still, I couldn't keep my mind from wandering, again and again, to the strange German.

The innkeeper knocked on the door, ready to help me lug my trunk down the steep, treacherous stairs. I followed behind. Yesterday, I was ready to leave this city behind me. Now, Thayer made me feel unsure.

I had to be smart. It was imperative I get out of here for the time being. Safety was found in short stays, rotating locations, and assumed names. This was my third time in the English-occupied city. I was experienced enough to know suspicion would soon cast its eye upon me. The English were suspicious of most, close to losing as they were. It was time to move on.

Out in the dirty street, the city was wide awake. People were everywhere, going about their business. The Red Coats were dotted here and there, bullying people as they passed by. While my trunk was loaded onto the back of the hired cart, I stole a look around. I was hoping to catch a glimpse of him, in a doorway or behind a lamppost. He was not there, and I dared not linger any longer.

Disappointed, I picked up my skirt, took the arm of my nondescript driver, and climbed onto the hard seat. This trip would be made with a pair of decent-looking, chestnut-brown mares. These were not the sad, half-starved creatures who assisted in my escape.

My dress matched the horses; an unassuming drab cotton without a single embellishment. I also wore a cream-colored shawl and a straw sun hat, secured under my chin with a bit of white ribbon. I had to look my part this morning, which was that of a plain, farmer's daughter.

The uneventful trip took two and a half days. We stopped at a couple of inns along the way to rest ourselves as well as the horses. The Boston Post Road was a well-established, well-used route. It was by far the best way to reach our destination. I used this time to think of anything other than Thayer. My mind went over the war, my past, and I even tried imagining what Benjamin was up to, but nothing could hold my attention.

Returning to Boston felt wonderful, and my spirits lifted immediately. I saw things with more clarity here. My heart felt lighter, in a way it only felt at home. A Hessian soldier locked in an affair with a Culper Spy was ludicrous. We could not be involved in any way. Entangling myself with the captain would compromise the others in the network. This could lead to its collapse, to the loss of this war. Nothing was more important than winning—nothing. Beautiful, bedroom eyes and strong, muscular arms would have to be forgotten.

By the time the kind, silent driver pulled up in front of my home, I realized just how exhausted I was. Bone-wearingly tired, I fished in my handbag for a little extra payment. Benjamin had already paid this man, but it never hurt to throw in a little more. The risk we all took was a great one.

Boston was a cleaner, more well-kept city than New York. The latter was still finding its way, and the occupation of Red Coats wasn't helping. Perhaps this was just my prejudice, as the pride I felt in this place ran deep. My city still had its obstacles to overcome. After the Siege of Boston ended with the English withdrawal in 1776, the people here were left to pick up the pieces. Recovery was sometimes slow going, but four years later, we were persevering.

I alighted onto the cobblestone street in front of the brick manor home I'd lived in for three years. Benjamin arranged a room for me on the second floor of this house, owned by Mrs. Greaves, a widow. There were two other tenants besides me; Mr. Arthur, a clerk, and Miss Wright, a schoolteacher. Luckily for me, they worked during most of the day, meaning I rarely saw them, as I was usually out most of the night. My job made friendships difficult.

Mrs. Greaves met me inside the door as the driver lugged my trunk up the stairs. She was an older lady, with wiry gray hair and the tiny bone structure of a bird. Her glasses sat perched at the end of her nose. It seemed they could fall off at any moment.

"Hello, my dear." She grasped my hands, leaning in to kiss my cheek. "How was your trip?"

"It was lovely. Thank you for asking." Mrs. Greaves was under the impression I had only gone just outside the city to visit my aunt. As far as I knew, I didn't have an aunt.

"Are you limping?" Mrs. Greaves stood back to look down at my feet.

"I sprained an ankle tripping over Aunt Elizabeth's cat. It's nothing."

She seemed to accept this as she patted my arm and said, "Well, you better go and rest it." Rest sounded like a story from a fairy tale, as I trudged happily up the stairs.

Once alone, shut inside my room, I slipped out of my dress, washed, and climbed into bed. It was only late afternoon, but my body was crying for peace. I needed to sleep for as long as I could.

Upon waking, I stumbled, disoriented, across the cold, wide pine floors and drew the curtain. The sun was just starting to set. Darn, I was hoping to sleep through the night, resetting myself with the dawn. Now, wakefulness would be my enemy, keeping me up all evening. I decided a proper bath was in order. After which, I would go to The Green Dragon for a meal and some ale. Perhaps, if I drank deep enough, the ale would lead me back to sleep.

The bath was delicious. If I hadn't been so hungry, I would've stayed in the warm water all night. My rumbling stomach propelled me into action. Tired of dressing so plainly, I selected my navy damask robe a la anglaise with delicate white lace at the elbows. There was not a lot of finery to be found in my wardrobe, but this gown was one of my best. I topped this with a white lace shawl and a matching cap. The late spring night was still unseasonably warm, so there was no need for a cloak.

The Green Dragon Tavern, a two-story brick building, was four blocks from Mrs. Greaves' boarding house. The tavern, a favorite with revolutionists, was where I met Benjamin a little over three years ago while working as a barmaid. The Green Dragon was also where the Boston Tea Party was planned, a very exciting time, which helped lead us to where we now were.

Walking by the low hanging tavern sign, a little spring in my step, I jumped up, giving it a tap. Not the best thing I could have done for my feet, but it made me smile, nonetheless.

Tonight, the bar was bustling with people and chatter, as usual. Bud, the portly proprietor, greeted me with a hug, seating me at a small table for two near the front window. I ordered a meat pie and a glass of amber ale, then sat back to take in the rest of the scene. There were several people I knew, who either nodded or raised a hand in hello. I smiled, nodding in return, glad to be back among my own.

I was startled when my eyes fell onto a stunning couple, both blonde, seated at a table near the back. Their beauty was astounding. Not only that, there was another quality which made them stand out, something I couldn't quite explain. I thought of Thayer, as he possessed the same shining, ethereal characteristic.

The couple was finely dressed. Their fine dress alone would make them the center of attention, but there was still something else. I seemed to be the only one to notice how different they were. To my eyes, it seemed obvious. The difference had nothing to do with their loveliness, and lovely they were.

The woman had delicate features and porcelain skin. A silk, baby-blue bonnet was pulled low over her left eye. She wore an ivory silk polonaise embroidered with wildflowers of blue, yellow, and red. The lace at her sleeves and neck was of the finest I'd ever seen. Lace of such quality could only be found in England or France. The man looked built for force, and was dressed in a rich suit of midnight black with a floral embroidered trim and lace like his companion. I was sure those were real diamonds shimmering on the buckles of his shoes. Surely, they were the richest pair to ever grace these walls.

I watched them, transfixed. I felt as if I should look away, but they were so dynamic. How was it no one else seemed to be paying them any mind? As I watched, their quiet conversation seemed to be turning into an argument. The woman tensed, leaning back. The man moved forward, reaching for her hand, but the woman turned away her head, placing her hands in her lap.

At that moment, she locked eyes with me. I didn't want to look away or pretend I was looking at something else, so I held her gaze. Her demeanor, before hard and cold, melted a little as she smiled. Her beauty was dazzling. The man was trying to win her attention back to himself, tapping on the table and clearing his throat. She rose from her seat, making her way toward me. Her companion crossed his arms, never taking his eyes off her for a second.

"Are you alone? May I sit?" she said, in a lilting French accent.

"Yes, please." I indicated the chair opposite. "Would your friend like to join us? We could pull over another chair."

"He can if he wants. My guess is he will prefer to sulk across the room." She sat with her back perfectly straight, hands clasped ladylike in her lap.

I smiled at her, feeling very much at ease. I was not usually comfortable with women, having always preferred the friendship of men. And I was not at my ease with the snobby, rigid, upper classes, but I could tell I was going to like her.

"Your accent is charming. What brings you to Boston?" I began.

"My cousin and I decided it was time for a fresh start, in a new country."

Cousin? I did not buy for one second the man was her cousin. The way his eyes smoldered as they watched her? Still, I supposed it was possible, but something told me these two were not related. I decided to mind my own business.

"I'm familiar with fresh starts. How long have you been here?"

"Only days. We have taken a house nearby. It will serve us, while we decide where exactly we would like to settle." She leaned forward as she talked, making me feel as if I had her full attention.

"I sincerely hope you decide to settle here. Parts of the country remain in turmoil. Boston is relatively stable and well-defended from the English."

"Yes, the English. One wishes they would give up and go home."

I laughed. "We all wish for this. I do believe, however,

the end of this conflict is drawing near."

"As does Alexandre." She moved her head in the direction of her companion, still watching her from across the room.

"How rude of me, it only now occurred to me to introduce myself. I'm Annie Monroe." I stuck out my hand, which the lovely lady grasped with a warm smile, although her hand was like ice.

"Millicent Mirabeau," she said, as we shook hands.

"Have you met many people yet? You must be received in the best circles." I gestured toward her fine gown.

Millicent looked down, smoothing the front of her dress. "I was, in France. I no longer have the desire to live such a superficial life. I would rather know people of real substance, with real lives."

"You'll find a lot of those types of people here. What part of France are you from? I've never been anywhere but the colonies. I imagine France to be a magical, beautiful place of rolling hills, fields of lavender, and magnificent chateaus."

She smiled, again looking down. "France is all of those things. I am from the Burgundy region. The lavender fields were my favorite childhood play place. I also lived in magnificent chateaus all my life."

My eyes widened. I was rife with curiosity. "Really? How wonderful. It must have been like a dream. Why would anyone want to leave all that to come to a place in the grip of war?"

She pressed her hands together in her lap. "It was less like a dream and more like a prison, at least for me."

"Oh, I'm sorry. That must be why you want a fresh start then. I'm asking too many questions, please forgive me." I bit my lip, annoyed with myself for being so curious.

She looked sad for a moment. "The prison of my life was only one reason for the fresh start. And don't worry, I am not offended by your questions. It is natural to be curious. I am interested in your life."

We paused our conversation as Bud set down my food and drink, his eyes glued to my new friend. "Thanks, Bud," I said with a giggle.

"Perhaps you could meet me tomorrow night? You can tell me all about Annie Monroe. My cousin is tired, and I should get him home." She inclined her head toward her companion.

"I would love to. Would you like to meet here?"

"Is there somewhere less crowded?" She looked around at the packed room.

"You could come to my boarding house. I'll make us tea. Tomorrow at four?"

"That sounds wonderful. However, I won't be able to come until after nightfall. Is that too late?"

"Not at all. I look forward to it."

I told Millicent my address and she stood to leave. The man she called Alexandre rose in sync with her, then met her at the door. The man never once looked at anyone else in the room. I looked forward to getting to know this mysterious woman. Having a female friend might be a nice change.

CHAPTER FIVE

Annie

Waiting until evening to see my new acquaintance seemed cruel. Patience was not one of my virtues. I was fortunate to have several chores which should keep me busy most of the day.

When Benjamin arranged for me to stay at Mrs. Greaves' boarding house, he also arranged for me to do some light housekeeping to help pay for my room and board. Benjamin did not want me to work in the taverns or anywhere else once I became a member of the network, preferring me to be available at a moment's notice. He provided me with enough pocket money to eat, with some left over to occasionally purchase new material for a dress.

Mrs. Greaves was a skilled seamstress, sometimes sewing a new dress for me in exchange for extra housework. This arrangement suited me greatly. I had the freedom I craved and enough work to keep me busy. Mrs. Greaves never questioned my sudden absences. She only made polite inquiries as part of conversation. I did wonder at times what her relationship with Benjamin truly entailed. Was she another piece of the far-reaching network? I believed she was, but I would never dream of asking either her or Benjamin. This was part of our code. The less we knew about each other's connections, the better.

The boarding house was a two-story, brick square which occupied an entire corner in a bustling section of town. The home was well-maintained with exceptional furnishings, many from Mrs. Greaves' childhood home in England.

My front facing room had a window looking down on the street below. I loved the view I had, making me feel I could always see who was coming and going. My bed was small but comfortable, with a firm stuffed mattress and colorful patchwork quilts made by Mrs. Greaves. She never wasted material.

The furniture came with the room; a solid maple chest of drawers, matching armoire, and a wing-back chair upholstered in a deep-blue cloth. The painting on the wall over the bed was a favorite; a ship caught in a storm. I often felt this painting was a depiction of my experiences; I was the ship, always at odds with the life around me. A large oval mirror stood over the chest, which also held a porcelain ewer and wash basin.

After tidying my room, it was time to get on with the rest of my chores. As I was dusting the parlor, a knock on the door startled me out of my reverie; a fantasy starring Captain Emmerich.

I opened the door to reveal a pretty, petite woman, standing on the stoop. She wore a white lace cap perched on top of her light-brown hair and swished the skirts of her cornflower-blue dress, as if she couldn't quite keep herself still.

"Hello, may I help you?" I asked. Her swishing brought a smile to my face.

"I'm looking for Miss Annie Monroe."

"I'm Annie," I said, opening the door wider. "Please come in."

The pretty lady stepped with a light foot into the front hall. "I'm pleased to meet you, Miss Monroe. I'm Betsy

Ross. Mr. Tallmadge sent me here with a little gift for you."

My curiosity was piqued. Ms. Ross didn't seem to be holding anything, not even a handbag. I had, of course, heard of Betsy Ross and the famous flag she presented to General Washington.

"Would you like to come in and sit? I'll make us some coffee," I offered.

"Thank you, but I can't stay." She reached into the pocket of her dress, pulling out a bit of cloth. She unfolded a small rectangle of red, white, and blue. I recognized it immediately.

"This is a miniature version of the flag I made for General Washington. Mr. Tallmadge asked me for several of these, requesting I deliver this one in person." She held it out for me to take.

I was in awe of the little flag. It was all of four inches long but represented everything I believed in. "It's beautiful, Ms. Ross. Thank you, I'll always treasure it."

We shook hands, then she went on her way. Refolding the precious bit of cloth, I placed it in my own pocket. Benjamin knew the importance of this symbol. He must be giving one to each of his spies. This meeting with Betsy left me invigorated, excited for the evening ahead.

It took me only an hour or two to complete my day's chores, which left me with too much time to myself until Ms. Mirabeau would arrive for tea. To pass the minutes, I washed the tea set again, then picked out the best cups. I could only imagine what the teacups Ms. Mirabeau was used to drinking from were like. Much finer than these, no doubt. She didn't seem the kind to turn her nose up, so I tried not to worry. She sat with me, after all. Although not poor in appearance, my dress last evening was in no way as fine as hers.

Thinking on this, I started to fret as to what I would wear for our late tea. I did have two very fine gowns. These had been provided by Benjamin for my rendezvous with officers and would be overdoing it for this occasion. I decided on my gown of deep-red damask. It was pretty and would do for the occasion. I asked Mrs. Greaves if I could borrow her garnet earrings, then went to lay out the dress to air.

As I pulled it from my trunk, my hand brushed the Ottoman dagger gifted me by my handler. I picked it up, holding it in my hand. As I did so, my mind was flooded with unwanted thoughts of Thayer.

I tried to tell myself it had only been a few days. Time would help me forget this German who had made such an impression on me. My heart started to beat a little faster as I thought about our kiss. I was not a stranger to intimacy, but he made me feel like a girl who'd been kissed for the first time. I had to be strong and push these thoughts away.

Before dressing, I removed the flag from my pocket, smoothing out the material on my bed. The question was, what would I do with such a gift? I would have to find a frame for it, so it could hang on my wall, always in sight. To tuck it away was out of the question.

Night fell by the time Ms. Mirabeau arrived at the front door. Mrs. Greaves and Miss Wright had retired early, while Mr. Arthur was out at the pub, so we were alone.

Millicent was again dressed like a princess in a cream silk gown accented by snow-white lace. She wore a simple, but valuable triple-strand pearl choker with matching pearl ear bobs. Her pouffed hair, a bit messy, was decorated with a single creamy feather. I figured this was understated compared to how she was used to dressing. She still managed to look like royalty. The fine silk of her gown alone was worth a fortune. As I helped her remove her ivory velvet cloak, I tried my best not to be self-conscious.

"Red is your color, Miss Monroe. It brings out the richness of your hair and the fairness of your skin," she said, after we greeted each other, and I showed her in. "What a lovely parlor; so warm and comfortable."

I couldn't help but giggle. "Thank you, but I'm sure

these surroundings pale in comparison to what you're used to."

She looked down. I had the feeling I embarrassed her. "I'm sorry," I said. It seemed I had a knack for making her uncomfortable. "I should have stopped at thank you."

"Don't apologize. You're not wrong. The life I lived in France was lavish, ridiculous even. I hated it. I have always longed for a simpler life."

"I understand. And now, you shall have it. Boston is the better for your presence."

Her face darkened, almost imperceptibly. She covered it with a placid, happy visage. "You're sweet. I shall have some version of simple, I suppose. I would much rather talk about you, Miss Monroe. Have you always lived in Boston?" she asked, taking a seat on the settee.

This was why I dreaded talking about myself. I had to keep key parts of my life secret. I shifted a little in my seat. "No. I was born and raised in Virginia. I came to Boston at sixteen to work in the taverns. I've been here ever since."

Her eyes widened. "Alone? Were you not afraid?"

I shook my head. "No. I was never bothered by men, if that's what you mean. Unless I wanted to be."

I appeared to shock my guest as her hand flew up to her mouth. A moment later, she dissolved into giggles. I followed until we were both laughing so hard, we were gripping our bellies.

"Miss Monroe, you're wonderful. I've never known a woman like you. Never have I lived without shelter provided by a man. How I would dearly love to. I'm rather envious of your independence."

"It's Annie. I like you too, Millicent. I don't have any female friends, other than Mrs. Greaves, so this is a treat. But surely, you could easily live on your own if you wished."

"You have a friend now." She smiled at me before continuing. "I, too, tend to be rather solitary. Alexandre is my only real friend, but now I have you as well. Perhaps one day I will attempt to strike out on my own. Now isn't a good time. Alexandre would be lost without me." She smiled a smile which wasn't exactly a happy one.

This was my chance to ask her about Alexandre. "Yes. Tell me more about your cousin. He's probably the second most gorgeous man I've ever seen."

"Second? He would be offended to the skies to not be your number one. Alexandre is my cousin and companion. It really is as simple as that. I do admit he is handsome. I call him Jupiter, for the Roman god. He loves the reference almost as much as he loves himself."

We laughed again, and she continued. "As much as I can laugh at Alexandre, I'm also deeply grateful for him. He has been a rock for me during this time."

"What time would that be?" I offered her a tray of spice cakes. She shook her head.

"Just this time of transition. I'll pour our tea. It's probably getting cold." She reached for the teapot.

Millicent poured out the tea with the grace of a duchess. As I took my cup from her, the tops of my fingers grazed her hand. It was ice cold although the room was quite warm, so warm my brow felt shiny with perspiration.

"Are you cold? Would you like a shawl?" I offered. I wondered if she was coming down with a sickness and felt a little nervous. I didn't have the luxury of being sick in bed.

"Oh no, thank you. I'm always cold. It is nothing." She smiled, sipping her tea.

I couldn't help but think this was strange. She looked healthy enough, more than healthy. Millicent's skin glowed with vitality. My mind wandered to what I would call the otherworldliness of herself and her companion. They were very much like Thayer, in their bearing and movements. Thayer was also cold to the touch. The frigidity of his body could be felt through his uniform. I shook my head. Benjamin had infected my mind with his superstitious foolishness. This woman was flesh and blood. She was also breathing, therefore, not a vampire. I giggled.

"What's funny?" asked Millicent, her eyes narrowed

slightly.

"You'll think I'm crazy, but it isn't me. Really, it's my friend who's the crazy one." I shook my head again at my silliness.

"I would love to share in the joke. Please tell me, nothing surprises me anymore."

"Well, this friend was recently showing me a box of his own creation. You won't believe me, it really is absurd. The box contained tools to slay...vampires."

Millicent dropped her cup, shattering it on the pine floor. Dark-brown tea spilled onto her dress and shoes. "I'm so sorry. How clumsy of me." She cut her finger, a drop of blood sliding down the side of her hand and put the wounded appendage into her mouth to stem the flow.

"Don't be silly. It's just a cheap cup. I'm more worried about your fine silk. Let me get you a rag."

I rose to walk into the kitchen. While there, I heard Millicent say, "Please don't concern yourself."

"Nonsense," I said upon returning, handing her a damp cloth. I swept the remnants of the cup off the floor while Millicent wiped off her gown.

"Here," I said, handing her a bit of clean rag from my pocket. "Wrap this around your finger."

"I beg your pardon, what finger?" She looked up at me with the most innocent eyes.

"Your pinky. You cut it on the broken porcelain. I saw the blood." I pointed to her finger, as if my gesture would explain everything.

She held up both hands. "No cut. You must have been seeing things in the confusion."

I knew what I saw; a good-size slice which started to ooze blood. My skills of observation have always been sharp, even before I became a spy. I took a step backward, refusing to believe what my senses were trying to tell me. Millicent rose out of her chair and moved two steps back herself.

"Annie, it's okay," she said softly.

"What are you? You can't be what I think you are." It was then I noticed something else about her. Her eyes had a glow reminiscent of a feral cat. Had the glow always been there?

Millicent pressed her hand to her forehead, closing her eyes. "I think I should go. I'm sorry if you were frightened. It was a mistake to think I could have a friend."

As she turned to leave, I felt a panic rise within me. I didn't want her to go. If she was what I thought, I was never in any danger from her. Thayer too, only wanted to protect me. Everything I thought I knew, everything Benjamin warned me of, didn't seem in keeping with the myths. At least, not with Thayer and Millicent. What else didn't I know?

"Wait. Please don't go. Will you sit back down? I want to ask you some questions. Please," I begged her, as I tightly gripped the broom handle.

"Are you sure? I don't want to scare you." She peered at me from over her shoulder, her golden hair beginning to come loose around her.

"I'm not scared," I said, standing straight, loosening my grip.

Millicent smiled, turning back to face me. "No, you're not. Only startled. What must it be like to be so brave?" she asked rhetorically, resuming her seat. "If I am to answer questions, then you must as well. There are some details I would like you to clear up about your life."

I nodded my assent as we once again faced each other.

"What do you want to know?" I asked first.

"You are hiding something. I want to know what it is."

I hesitated, unsure how much I should divulge to this creature. Then deciding I should be as forthright as I hoped she would be, I said, "I work for the rebels in the fight against the English. How, I can't say. In doing so, I would be compromising other people, not just myself. Please understand this must remain a secret, too much depends on this."

She nodded. "I understand. But how wonderful. Alexandre would be as impressed by this as I am. He loves a good revolution, or so he said when we arrived. What would you like to know about me?"

I looked down at my hands, thinking how best to formulate this question. There seemed to be no artful way to ask. "What are you?"

"What do you mean?"

"You know what I mean. I have come across another like you. He emanated this extreme power. You and Alexandre radiate the same strength. Also, the coldness. And, the cut on your finger. I know what I saw; it healed. I don't believe you can be human, but I can't quite make myself say what I really think you are."

She sighed. "Alexandre is furious. He doesn't want me to tell you anything. He says we will be made vulnerable."

"*Is* furious?"

"Yes. He can hear my thoughts. He can talk to me telepathically. Lucky for you, I enjoy irritating him and I think you can handle the truth, Miss Monroe. I don't believe you will try to harm us."

"I would never hurt you. Please… I just need to hear you say the words."

"You need to hear me say we are vampires? We are. I can't speak for this other person you mentioned, but Alexandre and I are immortal creatures, imprisoned by the night."

I sat back in my chair, looking into this woman's black eyes. I was speechless. I had nothing to say as my mind went blank. A few minutes passed, with Millicent remaining as silent as I was.

After a few moments, I found my voice. "Make me what you are."

Her eyes became sad and she looked down. "You don't want to be this, Annie. We are no better than monsters. And you, you are so noble, so brave. I would hate to see you lose yourself."

"I won't lose myself. What I will do is gain. Gain strength, speed. That is what I need, physical power to see this war through to the end. You can give me the advantage I require."

She shook her head. "I don't know. At any rate, I can't decide this on my own. Alexandre will have to make the final decision. He will have to be the one to do it. I am too new to this existence. Think on this. Consider what you are asking very seriously. I'll return tomorrow night."

Before I could open my mouth, she was gone.

CHAPTER SIX

Annie

In the blink of an eye, my world changed. Dozens of thoughts swirled through my mind. It was difficult to take in this new information. Everything happened so fast, it was hard to assimilate. Could I accept what I had seen? Been told as fact? There was no denying what I saw with my own eyes; the wound healing, the swiftness of her movements, the frigidity of her skin, and the fact she told me point blank what she was.

After cleaning, I slipped into bed. Sleep was going to be impossible, but I at least needed to rest. As I lay there thinking about the existence of vampires I became jittery with excitement. I could be one of them; strong like them, fast like them. Capture would be something I would never have to worry about again. Think of all I could do for the cause. Most of what I did took place under the cover of darkness anyway, so being limited to a nocturnal lifestyle would not diminish my effectiveness.

I could be Thayer's equal. His strength, his power, would no longer intimidate me. I could even see him, as often as I liked. I was more convinced than ever that he too was a vampire. Surely, he would be happy to see me no longer weak. I had to wonder why he himself had not shared this gift with me. I made a note to find out when next I saw him, which I was now sure I would. Maybe I could turn the tables and intimidate him a little. As unlikely as this was to come true, it still made me smile.

I fell asleep just as the sun was rising, waking again at dusk. I donned my navy damask, tying my lace fichu around my shoulders with trembling fingers. I was ravenous with hunger.

A hearty aroma from below set my stomach to rumbling. Mrs. Greaves had some delicious smelling stew simmering in the kitchen, of which I helped myself to a bowl.

"Oh, Annie. Good, I'm glad you found the stew. I was getting ready to give up on you eating this evening," she said, as she bustled around the kitchen, tidying up the already clean room.

"You must think me lazy. I've been sleeping. I've had a difficult time falling asleep since returning from my aunt's," I said in between spoonsful of the meaty stew.

Mrs. Greaves turned to me with what I could have sworn was a knowing look. "Of course, you're tired dear. You've done so much since coming here." She smiled before returning her attention to wiping the butcher block.

I didn't say anything but wasn't surprised. Benjamin wouldn't place me with someone he didn't trust. I finished my meal, then slipped outside to the porch to wait for my ethereal friend.

I sat there a long time, hours. Mrs. Greaves came to latch the front door and was startled to see me outside. "My dear, it's past midnight. Are you unwell or waiting for someone?"

"I'm just feeling a little warm. I'll come in soon and latch the door myself."

She looked wary but agreed.

After even more time elapsed, I at last heard the click of shoes on the cobblestone street. There was only one lamp lit on this block, but almost as soon as I heard her walking,

I saw her. Her blonde hair was uncovered, flowing as she walked. A black cloak, pulled around her, concealed whatever gorgeous gown she wore this evening.

I stood to calm myself before walking down the steps of the porch to meet her in the street. The annoyance I felt at being made to wait was lifted by the excitement pulsing through my veins. Still, I didn't want to seem too eager.

Millicent met my eyes without so much as the trace of a smile on her lips. "Hello, Annie," was all she said.

"Why do you look so unhappy? Where is Alexandre? Are you going to take me to him?" I asked too many questions at once, thwarting any attempt at coolness. This wasn't beginning the way I thought it would.

"I will take you to Alexandre. He would like to meet you. He knows you already through our last conversation but wants to ask you some questions. Before I take you to him, I want to impress upon you the finality of what you're doing." She stood straight, her face serious.

"I understand it will be final," I said, as I began to feel frustration. "Would Alexandre choose to make me what you are?"

"Annie, please. Let's sit for a moment." She moved toward the porch.

"I don't want to sit. I've made up my mind. I know what I'm doing." I really didn't but preferred to show no weakness. Millicent didn't seem to buy my confidence, as her eyes narrowed with suspicion.

"Do you? You know from this night on you will crave blood for an eternity? Warm blood, fresh blood. Blood from living beings. This is something you understand? Drinking blood from a human takes a lot of getting used too. You will even kill from time to time."

I had been so focused on the new strength I would possess, that I hadn't thought on this too much. Drinking blood did not sound appealing, I had to admit. Let alone blood from a warm, living human being.

"I didn't think about that. I'm sure I could do it, though.

Especially if blood is what it takes to survive." I dug my heels in, unwilling to let this chance pass me by.

"You will also be a slave to the night. Never again will you see a sunrise. Never again will you enjoy a walk on a bright, sunny day. You will have to give up your lodging here, to come and live with us. No one else can know what you are." She was making some good points against this decision. I was starting to second-guess myself.

"Why did you become this? Did you have a choice?" Again, I noted an intense sadness behind her eyes. A sadness she quickly blinked away.

"Let us sit, Annie. Follow me." She made her way past me, up the stairs of Mrs. Greaves' front porch.

Millicent looked over at me, still standing in the street, then patted the empty space next to her on the bench. She was stubborn, but so was I. As I continued standing in the street, a feeling of foolishness came over me. This was not the way to begin, not the way to get what I wanted.

Crossing my arms, like a child not getting her way, I went to her. When I was seated, she began.

"Very good. Now we can talk like civilized people. You want to know if I was given a choice. I was. My reasons for choosing this life were very different from yours. I lost everything that was precious to me; the man I adored and his baby. I no longer cared what became of me. But, I do regret it, Annie. Eternity stretches out before me like an endless sea of darkness. If I had remained as I was, I could have joined him eventually. As it is now, I may never join him at all."

I didn't know what to say. Before I could begin to form any words, Millicent spoke again. "You will never have a normal life. You will never marry, never have children. The people you know now will wither, die, and you will always go on. Make very sure this is the existence you want because it is a long one. Horribly long."

I leaned against the back of Mrs. Greaves' bench, my arms still crossed. "Will Alexandre change me, if I wish it?"

"Alexandre will change you, if you wish it."

"This is what I want, Millicent. I want to be like you, like Alexandre. I understand everything you've said. Yes, it will be a challenge. I'm sure there will be moments of regret, but there can be no guarantee in anything we do."

She looked off into the night for a long moment. "I would love for you to join us. If you're sure. And Annie, it doesn't have to be right now, we can wait a little longer."

"I couldn't stand to wait. Not when I know you exist. I'll get my things." I bolted up, off my seat and into the house, creeping to my room. I packed my few possessions as quickly as I could. In the end, I had one trunk of clothing along with a large satchel that contained my few toiletries, a silver-plated hairbrush with matching mirror, the Ottoman dagger, Betsy Ross's flag, and Benjamin's superstitious implements. I couldn't stand to part with anything given to me by Benjamin, so I tucked them away.

I took a piece of paper from the bedside drawer to write a goodbye note to Mrs. Greaves, which I left on the bed. She would be wounded by my leaving in this way. I hated to hurt her, but this was too important. My destiny seemed to be pushing me in the direction of these immortal creatures.

"How did you think you were going to get the trunk down the stairs by yourself?" I jumped at the sound of Millicent's voice, clamping my hand over my mouth to keep from screaming.

She picked up the trunk without so much as a sigh. Then, without any noise, took it down the stairs. I closed the door on my room, following her. Outside, Millicent shouldered the burden and said, "We better get off the street. This is sure to look odd to anyone walking by."

I was in awe of her strength. More giddiness swept through me at the thought that I would soon be this strong.

We walked side streets, zig-zagging through alleyways to keep us hidden. After what seemed like an eternity, we were striding up the front path of a beautiful brick home. We were now in the wealthiest section of Boston. The house was exquisite. At the grand door, she set down my trunk.

"This is your house? It's wonderful." I don't know why I was surprised. Anyone who dressed with as much beauty as Millicent and Alexandre would also live in a fine home.

The place was large, three times the size of Mrs. Greaves'; a grand three stories, not including the attic. The exterior was covered in russet-colored brick. The windows, there were so many windows, were trimmed in white wood, flanked on each side by black shutters. The fence was an object of great craftsmanship in black wrought iron, topped with fleur de lis finials. An ancient oak tree, perfect for climbing, shaded the front walkway from the light of the moon, its long branches dipping down like the arms of an elegant lady.

"It does its job. It was the fleur de lis of the gate which caught my eye," she said, opening the door and leading me inside.

I had seen homes as grand as this, occupied by English officers, but this didn't diminish the home's beauty in any way. Millicent walked across the large foyer, opened a pocket door, and stepped back, facing me.

The front hall was unlit. I couldn't make out much. The only thing I had any real sense of was the size and the high, vaulted ceiling.

"Please come in, meet Alexandre. Don't forget to tell him how wonderful he is," Millicent said, a sour look on her face.

"Very funny, Millicent," said a deep voice, booming from the room beyond.

I walked with some trepidation toward what must be the parlor. The room was large and bright. Everything was beautiful; a parquet floor of oak, a cavernous brick fireplace, and a recessed ceiling graced in the center by a chandelier of shiny bronze. The furniture was far simpler than the room called for; a divan of striped silk, two dark, wooden Windsor chairs, and a Turkish rug which didn't belong.

"We just moved in. The furniture came with the house,"

said Millicent. "I'll be changing it soon."

The enormous, blond man from The Green Dragon was sitting with his legs crossed on the divan.

"You must be Annie. Please come in and make yourself at home." Alexandre gestured to a seat across from him. He was dressed for a casual evening in dark-green pants and a white shirt, open at the collar. His black shoes were plain, with only silver buckles.

"So, my dear. You wish to join our little family. I know Millicent will be glad of a companion, other than myself." He paused, considering me. "It took me a long time to find her, and making immortals is not something I do lightly. She seems to think you would be a worthy addition. What do you think?"

"It's difficult to speak of one's own worth. I only know why I wish to be what you are. My value is for the two of you to judge." I then explained to these two beings, my involvement in the revolution. I emphasized how being a vampire would help me to be more effective. "I tell you this in confidence," I added when I had finished.

"Of course," said Alexandre, stroking his chin. "Who would we tell, anyway? You do know this war will not last forever? In fact, by all accounts, it seems to be nearing its end as it is. Becoming immortal is permanent, Annie. This will be your existence for a very long time, perhaps forever."

"I understand this. Really, I do. I've no real ties to this life. After the war is won, I will be able to move on without looking back." I thought of Benjamin and Mrs. Greaves, my only real friends in the world. Their lives would go on just fine without me. Besides, I could still see Benjamin after dark, as Millicent had visited me. There was no reason he should have to know.

Alexandre looked me over, then gazed at Millicent for a long time in silence. I sat patiently waiting. "I know how Millicent feels. She's become quite taken with you in a very short time. I can see why. I believe you are worthy to join us, Annie Monroe. You have a spirit I have never seen before. There are some details you must know first. Then, we can proceed."

Alexandre went on to tell me, in almost clinical terms, how the procedure would take place and how I could expect to feel through the process. He also warned me it may not go as planned. Complications could arise. If this happened, he would have no choice but to destroy me. This was disconcerting, but I thought the likelihood of something going wrong would probably be very low.

"Millicent, what did you experience?" I asked my new friend, knowing she had not been immortal for long.

She explained what Alexandre did to her and how she felt during and after the experience. It didn't sound bad at all. I told them I was ready to do it, right then. Any more waiting may have found me backing out.

Millicent moved off the divan, where she was seated next to Alexandre. I took her spot while she stood by the fireplace, watching with wide open eyes. Alexandre pulled me across his lap. My heart began to thud in my chest with wild abandon once I was in his grasp. I was like a child in his arms, my face toward the ceiling. He pulled the fichu from my shoulders, dropping it to the ground. I shivered, involuntarily, thinking I may need a minute more. But Alexandre was bending down to me, and I closed my eyes tightly. Two sharp teeth cut into the flesh of my throat. I couldn't help but gasp. The pain was intense but momentary.

Once he began to drink, I felt as if in a dream. Very soon after, the feeling of floating was replaced by panic. I wanted to pull away, to say I changed my mind. But it was too late. I felt no longer in control. Had I ever been? A warm, thick liquid was moving into my mouth, sliding down my throat. My first instinct was to reject this; to try to spit it out. I knew if I didn't finish this I would die. I swallowed mouthful after mouthful of what I knew to be Alexandre's blood. It was bitter, metallic and foreign. Thankfully, as quickly as it had begun, it was over.

For a moment, I continued to lie there as I was feeling all my senses sharpen, come into focus. Almost as soon as a feeling of power began to flex through my body, I was spasming. I felt an immense pain, such as I had never felt before. Every joint, every muscle, every fiber screamed in agony. I fell off Alexandre's lap, writhing on the ground at his feet. I felt soft, cold hands on my arm and face.

"Alexandre, what's wrong?" I could hear the panic in Millicent's voice.

"It's normal. I've seen this happen before. It will pass." I heard his voice as if through a tunnel.

Millicent pulled me to her, rocking me back and forth. "It's okay, Annie. You're going to be okay. Alexandre says it will pass. Stay with us." She continued to rock me, now petting my hair. I curled into a ball, pressing myself as close to her as I could, the spasms still moving through me. I was in too much pain to have too many thoughts. One thing kept occurring to me, over and over, "Don't die."

"Alexandre, where are you going?" I heard Millicent say above me.

"She's your pet. I've done my part. I'll be upstairs, if she dies." His footsteps faded away.

"Typical," muttered Millicent. "The sun is coming up soon. When it rises, you will sleep. Everything will be much better after that. I promise."

Moments later, as the pain subsided, I blacked out.

CHAPTER SEVEN

Annie

Softness surrounded me. Bodily pain seemed but a distant memory. The space around me was pitch dark, and yet I could distinctly make out every stick of furniture in the bedroom; a chair, an armoire, a braided rug with muted colors, dulled with age. The room was mismatched, like the parlor below. Lying still for a moment, I luxuriated in the smoothness of the bedding. The coolness of it felt like heaven against my skin. Never had I slept on a mattress so comfortable. I felt enveloped, protected.

The door opened, revealing Millicent wearing a black silk dressing gown, carrying a single lit candle in a small, pewter holder in one hand and a mug in the other.

"Well, you certainly gave me a fright. You look like a new person this evening, which I guess you are." She sat the candle on the seat of the wooden chair.

I felt so splendid I had forgotten what happened. Sitting bolt upright, I ran my hands over my face, neck, and body.

Millicent laughed. "Everything where it's supposed to be?"

Instead of answering, I leaped from the bed and ran to

the mirror. My appearance was no different. It was my senses. Closing my eyes, I could hear people talking on the street below. Their words were so clear they could have been in the room.

The sound of bugs skittering on the branches of the old oak tree, along with dew dripping from the bud of an open rose in the flower bed reached my ears. Opening my eyes, I took in the room. I could make out microscopic specks of dust entwined in the cords of the rug, the finely woven individual threads of Millicent's dressing gown. My legs swayed underneath me, and I braced myself against the wall.

"This feels incredible." I spun around. "What else can I do?"

Millicent was lighting the room's lamps. "You are now able to move with such speed, mortals will not register you. You can jump great distances, so far it will almost seem like flying. The three of us have the ability to communicate with each other through our thoughts. And, of course, you will be strong. Very strong. This strength will grow as you age in your immortality."

This was everything I needed to hear. All the strengths Millicent had listed would help me as a spy. There would be no thwarting me, no worry about capture, and I would complete one mission after the next with absolute perfection.

Just when I was beginning to marvel in the totality of my invulnerability, I felt it; a deep burning in the back of my throat. Clutching my neck with both hands, I turned my eyes to Millicent.

"I know. You're thirsty. I'll dress quickly, then take you to feed."

"Feed?" I croaked.

"Yes, dear. Did you not understand that part? It's difficult to wrap your mind around until you feel it, I know. Drink this, it will help until we can find you something fresher."

Millicent handed me the warm mug. I gulped down the

liquid, which was congealing and off-putting. It felt strange to drink blood, but it did help a bit. She made me go to her room while she dressed. "I can't trust you alone, not until you've learned to control yourself. If you run out and slaughter the town, you will put us all in danger."

"How long did it take you to control this thirst?" My throat continued to burn with an intensity I had never felt before. Would it always be like this?

"No time at all. But, according to Alexandre, I was not usual. I also didn't experience the pain you did."

While she dressed, Millicent told me the tale of the occurrences preceding her new life. She thought perhaps because she was already dead inside, the change was very different for her. The normal Annie would have felt for her in her pain. As it was, I was very preoccupied with the gnawing in my throat. After what seemed like an eternity, Millicent was dressed in a dark-gray, silk polonaise. Leaving her blonde curls loose, we went out into the night.

Alexandre was home but didn't want to accompany us. His excuse being Millicent would be a better teacher. I still wore my navy damask. Looking down at myself as we walked, I felt drab next to my friend. Even though she wore a gray gown with no embellishments, the fineness of the gown was evident, as always.

"I've already ordered new gowns to be made for you," said Millicent. "Remember, I can hear your thoughts now. I went to the dressmaker after I left you at Mrs. Greaves'."

"How did you know my measurements? And how could you have known I would join you?"

She shrugged her shoulders. "I just did."

The day had brought a rainstorm. We stood in a wet, dripping alleyway on dirty filth. I worried for Millicent's exquisite slippers, but she just laughed. "We are creatures, Annie. Such concerns are no longer a consideration."

The alley smelled of decaying garbage. This, combined with my intense thirst, made it difficult to concentrate. Millicent taught me how to open my mind, exploring the unconscious emotions of mortals nearby until I found one who was unclean, as she called it. After several tries, I had it. I probed the feelings of those around me.

"I have one," I whispered, licking my lips.

"Where is he? Take us to him. I want you to take the reins with this, Annie. You will need to know how to feed yourself, should anything ever separate us." She touched my arm to prod me along. I didn't much like the thought of being separated from her.

We walked with rapid steps, silent as the grave through the streets, until we came up behind what was another grand house. "He can't be here," I mused.

"Because he's a gentleman, he can't be evil?" She was right. I already learned this lesson many times throughout the war, yet it still seemed wrong.

Millicent ascertained the man was alone, teaching me how to do the same. We entered through the unlatched back door. Arriving at the door of a library, I saw the man sitting with his back to us. He was rifling through papers on his cluttered desk. The entire room was in disarray, as if the shelves had been ransacked. Books were strewn across the floor. Millicent had explained how this would go before we entered so I would be ready.

She silently approached the man, took his head in her hands, and met his eyes. He gave a start, about to protest, when he suddenly became quiet.

"What a strange ability. Do you know what it is about our eyes that can mesmerize human beings?" It felt strange to say *human being*, as if human beings were now something apart from myself.

"No. Now, Annie." She held him out to me.

I was ravenous. Without any grace, whatsoever, I jerked him toward me, tearing into his throat.

"Try not to make too much of a mess," I heard Millicent say through the delicious haze of the blood.

When I had drunk my fill, and the man lay dead in my arms, I dropped him to the ground. I only spilled blood on my dress. Not a drop had fallen onto the floor. When the wounds healed, just as Millicent said they would, we left the man where he was. She said it would seem as if he suffered a heart attack. That would likely be the end of it.

Back outside, I felt euphoric. Spinning around in a circle, I let the blood fill my senses. "What an amazing feeling." I was still thirsty, but the blood left me sated enough. I hoped it would last a while.

"Yes, I suppose it is. You will be thirsty again soon. It is like that, at first. As you settle into yourself, you'll be able to go longer and longer without blood. Alexandre only needs to feed every month or so," she said, continuing to walk ahead.

I stopped spinning, then caught up to her. "The things that man did, they were…awful. Must we always see into their minds?"

"I know. It's unfortunate, but the images we see while feeding are part of the deal. It doesn't get less painful, I'm afraid. Alexandre says it becomes easier to shield your own mind while feeding, but I have not yet been successful. He isn't the best teacher. I'm afraid he's unable or unwilling to answer many of my questions and I grow weary of asking. I grow weary of most things."

I reached for her hand, giving it a squeeze.

We spent the rest of the night practicing my new skills. Jumping to the top of a building, then leaping from rooftop to rooftop was my favorite. I felt so free, so light. This was what total freedom was. Was this how birds felt? I was meant for this. I was not meant to be caged in, told what to do. If only I could share this gift with Benjamin.

"Why does Alexandre not create more vampires? We could share this with so many other worthy people," I said.

"He says there can't be too many immortals roaming the earth at once. There must be enough blood to go around. This was probably the only question of mine he has answered. I asked him this just the other night, after leaving you with a broken teacup," she answered.

It wasn't until close to morning when Millicent and I were snuggled in my new bed for a chat when I began to think, once again, about Thayer Emmerich. I told Millicent all about him; how we met, the night in the cemetery, and the kiss.

"He seems interesting," she said. "I admit, it does sound as if he is immortal. Strange he's a soldier. His men must know what he is, otherwise, how would he hide it?"

"I had the same thought. You don't know him then?"

She laughed. "No, Annie. We don't all know each other. Alexandre is the only other immortal I know."

Alexandre moved into the doorway. "Speak of the devil and he shall appear. How are my girls this evening? Has Annie learned all she needs to know?"

"Yes, it was wonderful," I said. "Except for seeing into the mind of some odious man."

"You'll get used to it," was all Alexandre said about the topic. "Millicent, are you coming to bed?"

I turned toward her, my eyes wide.

"Not tonight, Alexandre. Annie still has so many questions."

Alexandre didn't look pleased with this answer. "Very well. Goodnight then." He shut the door, his tread receding down the hallway.

"I knew it!" I said, feeling triumphant.

"Yes, well, what else have I got to do? My love is dead, and I go on, for eternity. Alexandre has been wonderful. I care for him. That is all. You will find conventional social mores no longer apply to us."

I'd never been conventional, so this suited me fine. This gave me hope regarding Thayer. I'd see him again, and I would make him mine.

The next evening when I woke, Millicent was already up. I found her luxuriating in a bath smelling of lavender.

"You can come in, Annie," she called to me as I stood

in the hall. Vampires need to wash only to remove things like dirt and blood. Millicent loved her baths, and I too couldn't imagine losing the habit of a daily cleaning.

I opened the door, steam escaping around me. "I wanted to tell you I'm going to the camp. I have to find Thayer."

"If you must." Her head rested against the back of the tub.

I wasn't expecting it to be so easy. Millicent read this on my face. "You're a free individual, Annie. You may come and go, as you like. The only thing you must do is keep what you are from mortals. They cannot see you feeding, jumping, or moving too quickly. I think you know this. Promise me two things; be careful around this German vampire and feed before you go. I feel confident you are in control of yourself. You don't know what his true motives are. Keep your eyes and senses open."

I promised, kissing her on the forehead. I had only known this woman a few days yet felt closer to her than I ever had to anyone.

"Can I ask you a strange question?" I asked, before leaving the room. "Why do you not have servants? It seems to me, ours must be the only house in this neighborhood which does not."

"I would think the answer is pretty obvious, sweet Annie. Hiding what we are from human servants would be impossible. The only way to do it would be to find people whose loyalty we could buy. Even so, there would always be a risk. Better to just take care of the house ourselves. Although, Alexandre becomes quite the grump whenever I ask him to dust."

I laughed at the thought of these two fairy-like beings engaged in such menial tasks. I left her to relax in her bath in peace.

Still awaiting my new gowns, I put on my red damask. To hide the bright color, I covered myself with Millicent's black cloak.

Before I left, I did something I should have done the

night before. I wrote a letter to Benjamin, telling him I had taken up a new boarding situation with the address where he could deliver messages.

The camp was at least three days away by horse. Millicent said it would take me about three hours to get there with my preternatural speed. I would stay in the country, out of sight. Six hours of travel only left me with roughly four hours of darkness to find Thayer. This seemed plenty of time, but she cautioned me to pay attention and not get stuck in the middle of nowhere with no shelter for the day.

I was careful to do as Millicent instructed. Three hours later, I was skirting the camp. It appeared I was just in time. Men were packing up, readying to move on. The rebel in me wondered where they were off to. This was information I should pass along to Benjamin.

"What are you doing here?" I heard the unmistakable, deep German voice behind me. Shouldn't I have been able to sense him? I felt a flutter in my stomach, and a smile played on my lips.

I turned. "I had to see you, again."

His face was visible in the starlight, my new eyes helping me to see all the better. The woods were sparse, not dense. I was worried we would be seen from the camp. I took Thayer's arm and the two of us walked deeper into the trees.

Once we stopped at a comfortable clearing, he said, "You've changed. Was it your choice?"

"It was. I never have to worry about capture by my enemies again." I felt confident, bold even.

"Not mortal ones, anyway," he responded. "This is no life for one such as you, Annie. I wish you had stayed as you were."

This statement angered me. "Why? So, I could remain weak? Easily pushed around and scared? No, thank you. I have nothing to fear now."

"There is much to fear. Even for those like us. You are strong now, but there are always those who will be stronger."

This was not going how I thought it would. I hoped he would be happy to see me, perhaps pulling me into another time-stopping kiss. He wasn't pleased to see me and did not seem at all inclined to kiss me.

I looked down at the pine needles under my feet. "I thought you might be happy to see me again. After what happened when I saw you last."

"I am, although I should not be."

"Because I'm a vampire now?" I peered into his eyes.

"No, because I have a duty and you are proving a great distraction." He looked away, into the distance.

"You're on the wrong side, you know," I said with a hint of a smile.

"Perhaps. For me, this isn't about right or wrong. It's about doing what I must for my family."

"What does that mean?" I pressed.

"I can't explain. Not now. Anyway, we are getting ready to break camp and move on."

Shoving my hands into the pocket of my cape, I said, "I understand. I shouldn't have come."

"No, I'm glad you did. Albeit reluctantly."

I turned to go, but Thayer reached out and held onto my arm with gentleness. "We are setting up camp about two miles from here. My tent is safe from the sunlight. You could follow us, under cover, then stay with me for the day…if you like."

I smiled. Human, my heart would be fluttering, and my breath coming faster. As it was, nothing much happened except for a pleasant nervousness in my belly. "Yes, thank you for the offer." I made sure to send out a quick thought to Millicent, so she wouldn't worry.

Thayer gave me instructions, which I followed to the letter. I had to wait for the human soldiers to trudge their way to the new campsite. I remained out of sight while the men performed their tasks; unloading and unpacking the carts, erecting poles, and setting up. Three hours later, the time it would have taken me to return to Boston, I was being shepherded into Thayer's tent. This one much nicer than the one I was held captive in.

This was the tent of an officer. It was the size of a large room. A desk stood in the center, toward the back, along with two chairs. To the left was the bed, large enough for Thayer alone. There was also a washstand, a rug that covered the ground under our feet and four trunks, stacked off to the right. His possessions were very sterile, very military.

My focus, though, was almost entirely on the bed. It wasn't clear if we would be sharing. I hoped against hope we would.

CHAPTER EIGHT

Annie

"You can take the bed," he said to me after entering the tent.

This statement took me aback. I thought his invitation implied intimacy. "Where will you sleep? The dirt floor doesn't look too comfortable, even with the rug." I was hoping to break the tension with a little joke. I didn't.

"I'll be fine," he said without looking at me.

I was beginning to wonder if this powerful man was at war with himself. Why invite me to stay the day, just so he could sleep on the floor? I was sure he knew I could make it home before sunrise.

Timidity was unknown to me, so I asked, "Why did you want me to stay here with you? You don't really want to sleep on the floor, do you?"

He was still turned away from me, making it impossible to read his face, not that I would have been able to, anyway. All I wanted was to feel this man's hands on my body, his mouth on mine. He was making this more complicated than it needed to be. We were both adults, immortal adults, so I didn't see what the problem was.

"I wish you had never come into my life," he said. His words were worse than a slap in the face.

"I'll go then. I'm sure I can find cover for the day, somewhere." I moved forward. Before I could take more than two steps, Thayer was in front of me, blocking the way. His hands were balled into fists by his side, his shoulders tight with tension.

"I didn't mean that. You have me confounded."

"Yes, you did. If you're thinking this is a bad idea, you're right. We will likely never be on the same side. We are doomed from the start. I shouldn't have come here tonight." I continued to look into his eyes, refusing to be intimidated.

"I want you more than I can say. More than I've ever wanted any woman." His words, which before cut into me, now took me by surprise. At last we were getting somewhere. I could see his face, readable for the first time. His eyebrows were pushed together, as if he were anguished, but his mouth was parted expectantly. The man who was unreadable finally let his torment show.

Stepping forward, I grasped his lapels, rolling the fabric between my thumbs and index fingers. I kept my eyes on my hands, unsure of where to go from here. I didn't want to press him, but I didn't want to make it too easy to cast me out, either. Thayer helped by placing a finger underneath my chin, lifting my face upward. Seconds after our eyes met, he leaned down, capturing my mouth with his.

Reaching up, I slipped my arms around his neck, stretching up on the tips of my toes. As we kissed, I started to slide his jacket from his shoulders, fearful he would resist me. He didn't. Instead, he stood back, removing the jacket himself. Thayer turned me around, unlacing my polonaise, then my corset with speed and deftness. Desire took hold of me. As I faced Thayer, he took my face in his hands, kissing me deeply. Once freed from our clothing, we moved to the cot. Thayer's body was so beautiful, I wanted to kiss him all over.

After pushing Thayer onto his back, I began to kiss and touch my way down his body. "I wasn't finished with you yet," he said, caressing my hair as it spilled around him. He went from ice cold to red hot in seconds.

I looked up, smiling a mischievous smile. "You'll get me back in a minute, or two."

I gently grasped his thickness in my hand. Thayer sucked in his breath. I dipped my head down, taking him into my mouth. Thayer moaned as he continued to stroke my hair. Not long after, he reached down, touching the tops of my arms. "You need to come up here, now."

I giggled, working my way back up. Thayer flipped me over onto my back, kissing my neck and breasts. He was about to return the favor I had just given, but I had other plans. "I need you, right now," I breathed, gripping his backside and bringing my legs together behind him. Never had I felt such urgency to have a man. He was causing me to feel, continuing to unlock doors inside me. I wasn't sure I wanted to feel anything more than lust, but my surety was weakening by the moment.

Supporting himself with one arm and holding me with the other, Thayer pushed himself inside of me. We thrust against each other in perfect rhythm. He aroused me so deeply, it wasn't long before I was crying out in climax, joined by Thayer moments later. He lay on top of me, spent. My body felt like a delicious tangle of tingling nerves. I lacked any will to move. His cot was only large enough for one. He positioned me so that I was half on top of him and pulled the blanket over us.

"I'm not sure I'll ever be used to not having to breathe," I said. It felt strange to not be out of breath, to not feel physically tired.

"You are new yet. It takes a while to feel comfortable in such strange skin."

"Are you saying my skin is strange?" I smiled up at him and then nibbled on his pectoral muscle.

"Your skin is a delight." As he said this, he trailed his

hand down the middle of my back, sending chills all through me. That one simple movement ignited my passion for him all over again. We made love once more, before the coming of the dawn.

"No one will bother us in here?" I asked, feeling a little nervous and vulnerable in the tent. It seemed strange to me; the soldiers outside going about the business of the day, while we were holed up in here.

"We are safe. My men, human though they are, know their captain to be eccentric and savage. Any suspicions they have are kept to themselves. I suspect they know, as we can be a superstitious people. But they follow my orders to the letter and are well compensated for any inconvenience. Sleep now." He held me close to him, my fears melting away with the comforting woodsy smell of his body.

When I woke, still in Thayer's arms, I heard a commotion outside the tent. It sounded like arguing, though I was no closer to understanding German. My body stiffened.

"Annie, you must dress quickly. I am sorry to be so abrupt," he said as he extricated himself from the cot.

"What's going on?" I sat upright, pulling the covers to my chin.

"I'm not sure. I'm sorry, but you need to leave. It isn't a good idea for you to stay much longer. Although, I wish you could." He sighed, then reached for my dress, depositing it on the bed next to me.

It was hard to feel hurt when he was right. I couldn't stay in his camp. I knew this from the beginning. We were on opposite sides of this fight. The night and day we spent together would likely not happen again for some time. Perhaps, when this was all over, we could be together. I had never thought much about having a romantic partner in life, or eternity, as it was now. Thayer had changed that. I could see myself with him, in a way I never had with anyone else.

"I know. It was nice to forget all this for one night, at least."

He looked down at me as he pulled on his breeches. His eyes were warm and soft. "Yes, it was."

I dressed, then Thayer led me out of the camp. I was seen by a couple of his men, but they looked away, the fear of having their necks snapped probably forward in their minds. Once out of sight, I turned toward Thayer to say our goodbyes. His eyes were returning to their usual stoniness.

"That was fast," I said, feeling the doors inside of me beginning to shut. I wanted to feel close to him, not closed off.

He took my hand, kissing my fingers. "I hate this, Annie. I hate what I am, I hate what I must do. I don't care one way or the other who wins this war. I must do as my family commands. Those commands are in direct opposition to what you believe in. Last night was perhaps the most wonderful of my miserable existence. But I must put it out of my heart and mind. I'm sorry if this hurts you. I wish I was anything other than what I am."

"You can choose to be whatever or whoever you wish. A family that holds your feet to the fire in such a way doesn't seem like much of a family to me. You must do what you feel is right. You know where to find me." I felt my words would have more weight if I left at that moment. There was no point in prolonging our goodbye, anyway. Thayer was fighting his own demons. I could not force him to change, to turn his back on whatever this family of his was. He would have to decide for himself what his future held.

My anger mounted as I made my way back to Boston, helping me to make record time. It couldn't have been much past ten when I slipped in through the back door of my new home. I walked down the hallway, heading to the main staircase.

"Our rebel returns," Alexandre called out from the parlor.

I froze where I was, not really in the mood, but decided

to play nice. These were now my people, my family, and I would have to act like it.

"Good evening, Alexandre," I said, entering the parlor. "Where's your better half?"

Alexandre chuckled, saying, "Out and about. She told me you were off to see a man. Go well?"

"It started off great. The ending, however, left a lot to be desired." I wondered if I should sit, try to make conversation. This man who I now called my maker was completely unknown to me. He seemed to have zero interest in talking or getting to know me.

"Endings usually do. I am sorry to hear it, but you seem a uniquely resilient girl. I'm sure you'll bounce back just fine." He was reading a book, not bothering to look at me. I glanced at the spine; *The Metamorphoses* by Ovid. If I remembered correctly, this work referenced Julius Caesar. I very much wanted to ask Alexandre about this but didn't feel the time was right.

"I'm sure I will. If you'll excuse me, I'll just go freshen up."

Alexandre nodded.

His comments irritated me, although he wasn't wrong. I would be fine. There was something odd about Alexandre. Something just below the surface I couldn't name. He was very likable, but not quite genuine. I wondered what Millicent saw in him, then remembered how he helped her after her heartbreak. Millicent was so much his opposite. The woman was moody. In the few short days I had known her, I had seen her rollercoaster of emotions several times. But, she was real. She wasn't hiding anything. I was disappointed she wasn't here to talk to.

I decided to take a long, hot bath. Perhaps I would stay in there the remainder of the night. The last thing I wanted to do was think about Thayer, so while I washed in my rosewater-scented heaven, I tried to put him out of my mind. Instead, I thought about the cause, and what my next mission could be. I was excited to use my new powers in the completion of my next task. I hoped it would be something big, something noteworthy. Flexing my new metaphoric muscles was just what I needed to feel like this change was worth the sacrifice.

I wondered if Benjamin would give me another easy assignment. If only I could tell him what I'd become. I wondered what he would do. Would he try and stake me with one of his pointed wooden sticks? Maybe he would shoot me with a silver bullet.

Wrapping myself in a blanket, I emerged from the bathroom. A note had been pushed underneath my door. It was from Benjamin. I wished Alexandre had knocked to tell me it was here. This was what I had been waiting for. My chance to show off my vampiric brawn had come. With trembling fingers, I opened the note.

Annie, I'm confused as to why you left your situation with Mrs. Greaves. The lady was beside herself at your sudden departure. I assured her you are fine. I hope I was correct. Knowing you the way I do, I'm sure you are awaiting your next assignment with bated breath. However, we have suffered a setback and all plans are on hold. The book has been stolen. You know what this means. Stay safe and out of the way, for now. Your friend, B.T.

This was alarming. The book to which Benjamin referred was the Culper Code Book. I was sure this was the volume I saw in his room the evening after my capture. This meant it was stolen between then and now. We were all compromised. The tome contained the code names of every spy in Benjamin's network. If whoever stole the book was able to break the code, those people were doomed.

I was no longer worried for myself, but for my fellow spies. They were all human and vulnerable. The loss of the book put them in greater danger than ever. It crossed my mind that Thayer may have something to do with this. He was in New York the same night I saw it. His excuse for being there had been to check on me. Was he lying? I felt a little sick to my stomach and sat on the edge of the bed.

If Thayer was watching me, he saw me meet with Benjamin and then go to his room. I led him straight to my friend, straight to the Culper Code Book. Had he been using me this whole time? Using me in an indirect way for information, just as I have used countless others? Would he have slept with me if he already had the precious journal? The last piece didn't seem to fit unless he was just using me for pleasure. And why not? He already had the book.

My blood began to boil. Feeling murderous, I was now convinced he did have it. I would find Thayer, then rip out his throat. I'd made a mistake. I could not allow myself to have real feelings for anyone during a time of war. Thayer knew this. He reminded me all along. Over and over he talked of his duty. He was right. He had his duty and I had mine. I would not forget it again. At least Benjamin was not hurt in the acquisition of the codes. I was, at least, grateful for this.

CHAPTER NINE

Thayer

The night and day spent with Annie were the most wonderful twenty-four hours of my existence. I had fallen hard for the woman. Never had I so much as dreamt of living a normal life, with a woman I loved and who loved me in return. But I dreamt of it now. I wondered if Annie was thinking the same. Even so, a dream it would have to remain. Emilia would never allow me to be involved with a vampire who was also a Culper Spy. My only job was to ensure the English remained in power here.

This was a job which was becoming impossible as the English lost more ground every day. Emilia didn't seem to realize how close the English were to losing. She remained stubborn, refusing to give up their position. Emilia always reminded me how a conquered people were easily controlled, making them a trouble-free supply of blood for our kind. Sheep didn't question, they accepted. This was why she was so dead-set on the English winning. The Red Coats thought they hired mercenaries. The Hessians' real reason for being here was much more insidious.

I knew this. I never questioned Emilia or my role in the

family. The ties which bound the Russian Romanovs to their German relations ran deep. I was always a good soldier, doing what she ordered without question. My life was regimented, ordered.

Annie began to obliterate everything I thought I knew to be true, as she unraveled my need for absolute order. I considered the vampires who changed her. They must not believe it necessary to keep the populace under the control of England, so why should I continue to act as a puppet?

Still, Emilia Romanov frightened me like no one else ever had or could. She was cold, ruthless, and calculating. She controlled the family with an iron fist. She was never questioned, not once that I knew of in all my one hundred years of life. I, myself, was always subservient, never questioning. I was beginning to think I didn't know what I was doing.

Making love to Annie while the Culper Code Book was tucked away in my trunk was a betrayal she would never forgive. I wanted to be honest with her; to give her the book had even crossed my mind. If I had, we would both have hell to pay. As much as she was beginning to mean to me, I knew in my heart we would both be better off if we never saw each other again. Emilia would go after her, along with her new family. My inner torment was almost unbearable. Was this how humans felt? Weak and unsure?

After Annie left, I stood watching her for a long time. I ached to call her back but dared not. One thing for sure, she was untrained. She left me the extra burden of shielding her mind as she retreated, as well as my own. Emilia was waiting for me back in the tent. With great reluctance, I turned away from Annie, back toward what I knew.

Standing just outside, I composed myself, steeled my will to face the only creature who struck me cold with fear.

"What are you waiting for, Thayer? Have you been naughty?" Her icy voice cut through the thick canvas of the tent, piercing me like a dagger.

I pulled back the flap, facing her, my visage as placid as

ever. "Emilia, how was your journey?"

"It gets longer, harder. My age begins to weigh on me, Thayer. Alas, there is no rest. Not when I must keep a watchful eye on my progeny. I worry so." She sat in the chair behind my desk, looking like no more than a child, but with an air of command that would make General Washington jealous.

You worry less about your progeny and more about yourself, I thought. "Of course, Emilia. You have come all this way for the book. Allow me to retrieve it for you."

"No need," she said, pulling the small notebook from the folds of her black crepe gown, the only color she ever wore.

Her heavy, dark gown, devoid of any ornamentation, only made her appear smaller. If she shrank any more, she would be swallowed by the enormity of the skirts she was surrounded by. Her thick black hair was pulled sharply back into a braided bun so tight it had to be uncomfortable. This added to her severe appearance. She may have been short, delicate even in stature, but I knew how powerful she was. There was a reason why she had never been challenged. Her core was ancient. She killed without effort, without remorse.

"Wonderful. Hopefully, it will give you the information you seek." I stood in front of her, at attention, my trained mind locked to her.

Emilia didn't respond. Instead, she looked around the tent from the chair behind the desk, taking in every detail. Her eyes stopped on the cot.

"Your bed is in shambles. It seems out of character for you to leave it in such a state. Where were you when I arrived?" She looked at me with her cold gaze. She knew the answers to her questions already. Even though I was skilled at shielding my mind, the others in this company were not. Lucky for me, the soldiers who saw Annie this evening were not the men who captured her, so wouldn't know her as the spy who escaped.

"I had company. I escorted her away from the camp as

you were arriving," I answered, matter of fact.

"Of course, you can keep whatever company you like. If it doesn't interfere with your purpose, that is."

I couldn't help but cringe a little, as she continued. "Does this woman live nearby? There is nothing around I know of, except trees and bugs."

"I believe so. To be honest, I wasn't interested enough to find out." It took all my inner power to keep my face completely blank.

"Hmm," was all she said. Looking down at the book, she added, "In any case, you did well acquiring this. What I would like to know right now, is how you managed to let a spy slip through your fingers."

"I'm not sure how it happened, to be honest. She befuddled the entire camp. I believe she may have been a witch." As the lie left my lips, it didn't sound all that far-fetched.

"Interesting. I haven't crossed paths with a witch in some time. I'll have to investigate this more. In any case, I shall let you know what we discover once we break the code. You know I detest the wilderness. There is no reason to stay longer. I'll be in the city while the book is being deciphered."

I nodded, relieved that she seemed to accept my excuse.

What she would do to these spies, once discovered, was not a question. Emilia would end them, without hesitation. I worried for Annie. I told myself she was immortal now and could take care of herself. She would also have the protection of her maker and immortal family, whoever they were. I had to hope he or she was powerful enough to thwart Emilia. My reason was at odds, and I could see this.

"Actually," Emilia said, as she rose from the chair, "since I'm here, and you would probably like to appease me for losing the spy you captured..." She paused, waiting for me to acknowledge her.

"Whatever I can do, you know that," I said, not allowing any emotion to cross my face.

"There is a regiment of our people not far from here.

The entire company has caused me several embarrassing problems. Captain Klein has been disobedient one too many times. They must go," she said with the simplicity of a child.

"The entire regiment," I repeated, not so much as a question, but a statement. I didn't think I would get off so lightly for letting Annie escape. Now I was facing my punishment; the extermination of an entire group of men. Killing was not a problem for me, but this mindless group murder was distasteful.

Emilia didn't respond, or so much as nod her head as she stood in front of me. She often tested her subordinates in this way. Captain Klein was immortal, but not a family member; therefore, he was disposable, of little value to Emilia if he was disobeying orders.

"I'll do whatever you wish, Emilia, as always." I really had no option but to comply with her wishes. Rarely did Emilia put a member of the family to death, but it wasn't unheard of. Of course, I would do as she asked.

"Let us be off then." She snapped her fingers at me like a dog.

Moments later, we were heading through the pine trees in the direction of Captain Klein's camp. It didn't take us long to arrive. Emilia, with me one step behind, strode like a demon of the night, straight to the captain's tent. The soldiers had seen her before. They knew better than to try to approach her. Many scrambled out of the way, thinking the privacy of their own tents would be enough to keep them safe.

She lifted the canvas flap, entering immediately. Emilia did not have to announce her presence to anyone.

The captain, lounging on his cot, snapped to attention. "Ms. Romanov. What a happy surprise." Captain Klein looked anything but happy. He seemed rattled. "Please tell me how I can be of service." He was nervous, and there was a twitch to his eye. I could see his muscles tense beneath his uniform. I felt a little sorry for the man who had only seconds left to live.

"Captain Klein," started Emilia. "You've disappointed me greatly. You will be dealt with at once."

The captain began to protest, but there was no point, nor any time. In a flash, making no sound at all, Emilia had him on his knees in front of her, his skull in her delicate hands. A moment later, I heard the crunch of bone on bone, as Emilia pressed her hands together. She crushed the captain's brain between her fingers with ease. Once released, his body toppled over to the side, falling over with a dull thud. Emilia walked over to the man's cot, so she could wipe her hands on his blanket. When she turned to me, I had to fight to keep my face stony.

"Now, for the rest. We will drain them all, then leave them as they are. It will look as if an illness made its way through camp. This tent, we will burn."

"Should we not let the men live? Place someone else in charge? It seems such a waste of precious manpower." I hoped to appeal to her sense of pride. She wanted to win the war, and to succeed, they needed men. It was worth a try.

"I've made my decision. This regiment is worthless, a drain on resources we need for soldiers who can fight."

There would be no reasoning with her. I left the tent, ready to get this over with.

An hour later, back in my own camp, Emilia long gone, I felt a sickness in my belly which was foreign to me. I couldn't help but wonder what Annie would think of what I just did. Yes, they were her enemies, but she would not have approved of such senselessness. I walked over to the cot and began to make my bed. Pulling up the blanket, I caught Annie's warm rose scent. Holding the cloth to my nose, I inhaled. This woman would be my ruin.

Annie

Anger emanated through my bones, pulsing through me like a living thing. Before dawn, I slipped out of the house alone. As Millicent taught me, I found myself a deplorable man who made a good meal. My hunting skills improved each time I set out.

Alexandre left me alone all the time, and Millicent had not returned. Since he didn't seem upset or worried, I concluded this must be normal. The relationship these two shared was odd, to say the least. I couldn't wait to tell her everything; my encounters with Thayer, the stolen spy book, and my tidy meal. I felt she would be proud of me for my feeding skills, at least.

After eating, I returned to my room to plot my revenge on Thayer. I would get the book back. Making him pay for how he used me was also in the cards. I fell asleep with the dawn, fully clothed, various forms of torture playing out in my mind.

When I woke the next evening, Millicent was sitting up in bed next to me. She looked radiant, as usual, in a silk chemise visible through an open white velvet dressing gown.

"Good evening," she said, a sweet smile on her lips. "Alexandre said you came home from your excursion in a less than desirable mood. His words. Want to talk about it?"

"I've been dying to tell you everything. Where have you been?"

"As Alexandre would say; here and there. Really, I haven't been anywhere of note. I've been wandering the streets alone. I spent the day in the cellar of an abandoned house on the outskirts of the city. Remind me to not do that again. I just couldn't bring myself to come home."

"Why?" I sat up, placing my hand over hers.

"I get so sad, Annie. So sad I feel like I want it all to end. Alexandre doesn't like it when I'm so melancholy, so I take long walks. Sometimes days' long."

"I'm sorry. What can I do to help you?"

She leaned in, pulling me into a firm hug. "Nothing. Just knowing you're here and you care helps more than you know. Now, tell me everything."

After I concluded my tale, Millicent stared at me with her mouth open for a few seconds. "He did that to you? He was intimate with you, knowing he had already betrayed you?" All I could do was nod. "Oh, Annie. You poor thing, you must feel terrible. We will make him pay for this. What do you want to do?"

I smiled. I had only been with her a short time, but already she was on my side.

"How can you smile? Aren't you heartbroken?" she asked. Millicent was very sweet, and a bit naïve, no matter what she said about social mores.

"I am hurt, I'm upset. But heartbroken? I'm not sure. Anger is foremost in my heart now. I was beginning to care for him, but to be heartbroken, you must be in love. I wouldn't say I was in love, not yet."

"Well, hurt and upset is enough for me to want to rip his eyes out. What do you suggest? Do you want to include your contact, Benjamin, in our plan?"

I shook my head. "Definitely not. Benjamin cannot be hurt. I would never forgive myself. I think we take a direct approach. We go to him, demanding the return of the book. He must assume by now that I know. A detail like this means we lose the element of surprise. He will, at the very least, be expecting a visit from me. I see nothing wrong with giving him what he expects for now."

"Do you think he will give it back? Surely it won't be so easy."

"It won't. Will Alexandre help us? His strength will be helpful." I jumped out of bed and started pacing. "We stash Alexandre, then confront Thayer to return the book. If he holds fast, which he will, Alexandre can dash in to help us incapacitate him and snatch the book."

Millicent's eyes were wide, but her mouth was smiling.

"How thrilling."

I laughed, falling over on the bed.

"I've never done anything like this. Well, except the time I set fire to my chateau. After that, this is the most dangerous thing I've ever done. Alexandre will do it. He can deny me no request. We're sure to win. The book is as good as in our possession already." She launched herself off the bed.

Alexandre wasn't thrilled but agreed to help. "If I had known the problems changing a spy would bring to us, I would have refused," he said, right before agreeing to our plan. Millicent was right, he could refuse her nothing.

It was too late in the evening to begin our journey. Millicent and I tried to while away the hours the best we could. She taught me how to play whist. Alexandre even joined us, cheerfully, for a hand. Then, I rummaged through her wardrobe of incredible gowns. Her jewels would put the Queen's collection to shame. Millicent fastened Marie Antoinette's sapphire bracelet onto my wrist, but I didn't dare wear it for long.

As dawn approached, she kissed me on the cheek before retiring with Alexandre. "Sleep well, sweet Annie," she said. "Tomorrow morning, at this time, we will be tucking ourselves triumphantly into bed."

I hope so, I thought, right before everything went black.

CHAPTER TEN

Annie

Readying myself for the evening's events, I was a tangle of emotions. I brushed my thick dark hair until it shined, then styled it into a neat pouf. I may have been angry, but I couldn't deny my need to be desirable to Thayer. He hurt me, there was no question. But could I really say he betrayed me? I knew his aims, just as he knew mine. I never told him anything about the book. He would have found it, with or without me. At least, this was what I told myself.

There was, of course, another sticky truth. Thayer must have known he would be putting me in danger by taking the book, yet he took it anyway. If he had indeed been the one to steal it, which I believed he was. Therefore, he was okay with not only putting me in danger, but the other spies in the network, as well.

I supposed I was hoping he would have a change of heart, throw down his Mitre Cap, joining me in the revolution. What a foolish woman I was. My convictions were not malleable, so why should I have assumed his were?

Just as I was ready to go downstairs, Millicent swept in, looking as if she were ready to fill her dance card at a ball.

She shined from head to toe in silk and diamonds.

"My friend, you look beautiful. Do you think you may be dressed a bit too fancy for what lies before us? We will be traveling through woods with branches, snagging your lovely dress. The color too may be a little bright," I said, as gently as I could.

She looked down at her yellow silk, sack-back gown, embroidered with golden flowers and leaves. Fine lace peeped from her neckline and draped from the elbow-length sleeves. Diamond earrings shone from her earlobes. As she dipped her head, I could see the white feathers she had placed in her signature messy pouf with artful care.

Millicent looked at me, her brow knitted together. "Perhaps. Something plainer? The dress I wore to show you how to hunt?" she asked in all seriousness.

"Yes, come with me." I took her hand, leading her back to her room. "I think the gray silk will do quite well. Perhaps the feathers and earrings should stay here. I would hate for you to ruin your feathers or lose a diamond." Millicent wasn't used to skulking about in the woods at night.

I left her to change, then went to find Alexandre. He was waiting, impatiently, in the parlor, tapping his fingers on the arm of the divan. "We need to get going, you know? We want to give ourselves plenty of time, so we don't get stuck in the dank forest. Sleeping underground is not fun, I can assure you. What is taking so long?"

"Millicent needed to change. Don't worry, we will have plenty of time. I know exactly where we're going."

Once the three of us were dressed and cloaked for the night, we were ready to set off. By this time, I had begun to doubt this mission would be at all successful. Millicent was eager but didn't know the first thing about battle tactics. Alexandre only cared about finishing his book. The only reason he came at all was to keep an eye on his treasure. Still, I had to do something. Sitting on my laurels was not in my nature. So many lives depended on it. If it was within my power to retrieve the book, I must. Feeling fearful I would succumb to my feelings for Thayer, I steeled my heart as best I could. This was going to be the most difficult part.

Halfway to our destination, Alexandre asked, "Has anyone figured out how we are all going to sneak into this German vampire's tent? I know we vaguely discussed this, but did we come to a determination? Even if the other soldiers are human, this will be difficult to manage."

I pinched my nose between my fingers and closed my eyes. He hadn't been paying any attention, but he had a good point. Surely, we would be noticed. By myself, I may have managed to sneak in. For these two tall, blindingly beautiful beings, sneaking in seemed a lot less likely. We continued to brainstorm on the way. In the end, it was decided I would go in, asking Thayer to talk with me in the woods outside of the camp, feigning discomfort at being in the enemy base for a third time.

By the time we arrived, I was having serious doubts about our so-called plan. However, it was too late to turn back.

Peering into the camp from the trees beyond, it was clear night had settled in. Most of the men were asleep, with a handful on guard or milling about, which was good for us. Leaving Millicent and Alexandre, I crept my way toward the tent. I paused to stand outside for a moment to ascertain if he was alone. The moment I was fully inside, Thayer was next to me. Feeling like a fool, I cursed myself. He could feel my presence. Why was this not something Alexandre thought to share with me? I was supposed to be stronger, not weaker.

"What are you doing here?" he whispered, spinning me to face him. "You can't be here now."

Our bodies were close, and I could feel the tension from his body like a live wire—he practically shook with it. *Steel yourself, Annie.* I had to say this to myself a couple of times before I could shake his arms from mine and force my legs to step backward. I looked him hard in the face. "Where is the book?" I demanded.

He continued to look at me for several seconds, his face unreadable. "I don't have it."

"You must think I'm an idiot. Of course, I expected you to deny it." I cast a glance around, hoping maybe he was stupid enough to leave it in plain sight.

"Why would I deny it? I have not lied to you, Annie. Not about anything. I have only omitted certain details."

"It's a pretty big detail. You made love to me in this tent, on that cot, after you had taken the book." It was a statement, a statement I expected him to explain. "How could you do something so loathsome? You placed me and so many others in mortal peril."

The plan had all gone to hell in one moment. The game had been to lure Thayer out. But, if the book wasn't here, as he claimed, this was now pointless.

When Thayer didn't offer further commentary, I said, "Explain. Explain to me how you could do such a thing."

For the first time since I entered the tent, he looked away, unable to hold my gaze. His stare drifted down to the floor, as if he were ashamed. "It shouldn't have happened. The fault is mine. I apologize for bringing you here. I allowed myself to feel too much for you. This compromised my sense of duty. I was truthful when I said it was the best night of my life. But it can never happen again. Please forgive me for hurting you. This was not my intention. I have no excuse for taking the book. I was ordered to take it and I did."

"You must think me a simple child. You didn't hurt me. In fact, I was worried it would be you ending up with a broken heart." I lied the best I could. He had hurt me, more than I wanted to admit, but my pride couldn't let him know my true feelings.

His face changed, and he looked confused. "What do you mean?"

"I mean, I was only interested in a little diversion. You don't think I would seriously have feelings for a Hessian, do you? I admit you were fun, but to think anything more would happen is laughable. I do like a little danger with my sex."

Thayer's sleepy eyes opened to an extreme I had yet seen. The shock on his face was clear. "I see." He recovered quickly. "You were playing with me. I should have realized a spy can never be truly sincere."

His words hurt me as much as his actions did. I would not let my face betray anything. I sensed I had hurt him, too. "You were not sincere either. There is no point in talking of this any longer. The only thing important to me here is the book. You said you don't have it. Where is it?" I asked.

"You'll never be able to retrieve it. Consider the Culper Code Book lost forever." He began to turn away.

"I can't do that. The lives of my fellow patriots are at stake. I will stop at nothing to retrieve it, and I'm not alone. Where is it?" I fisted my hands into the sides of my dress to keep from strangling him.

"In the hands of someone you could never defeat, Annie. Stop this now and go back to Boston. I suggest you forget the book ever existed."

"If you knew me at all, you would know to save your breath. Who is this someone? Tell me, Thayer." It was all I could do to keep my composure.

Thayer walked over to one of his hard, wooden chairs and dropped himself down like a stone. "Why must you persist in this? She will destroy you. Annie, you are nothing to her. She will kill you as easily as swatting a fly."

"I know you can't possibly understand, but I have to try. I'm not alone in this, and my new companions will help me. Please, Thayer. Tell me who she is."

Defeated, he shook his head, shoulders slumped. "Her name is Emilia Romanov. She is the matriarch of the Romanov family and has been for millennia, possibly longer. I know no one who is her equal in age or strength."

"The Romanovs?" I asked, unfamiliar with this name.

"The Romanov line is that of Catherine the Great. Emilia is the matriarch. She rules from the shadows."

Now Catherine's was a name I was familiar with.

"How are you connected to them? What possible interest could a Russian family have in the outcome of this fight?" At the very moment I was asking Thayer these questions, I heard Alexandre, clear as a bell, in my head. *It's time to leave, Annie. This is over.*

I ignored him, repeating my questions to Thayer.

"I was a blood relative to the Romanov family as a mortal. I came under Emilia's notice as a young man. She thought I would make a good soldier for her, and she hasn't been wrong. She only changes a select few. The few she chooses must be of her line and must obey her completely. As for her interest in this political matter; a controllable people are a people easily directed and fed upon. Or so, she always says. Rebellious, liberty-minded individuals are not sheep effortlessly led to slaughter. Her only interest is preserving the food supply."

I felt disgusted. A shiver crept down my back. I too was a creature, like this woman. But I respected life, only feeding from the evil among us. This Emilia Romanov did not sound like someone I would like to get to know. She would wipe out every single person listed in the Code Book. Of this, there was no doubt.

"Where can I find her? She must be nearby."

"You still insist upon this crazy scheme? Even after what I have just told you?" Thayer stood, moving in front of me.

"I do. I must at least try. For someone who is always speaking of his duty, I would think you of all people would understand." I hoped this argument would appeal to him.

Thayer lowered his head. "You can find Emilia in New York City. She has a townhome there, near the Hudson River."

"Thank you for the information." I moved around him to leave, feeling there was no point in saying anything else.

"Annie, wait. Please, think this through carefully before proceeding. You may hate me, but I do not feel the same. I would be saddened to hear of your failure."

I couldn't bear to turn around and look him in the face. My feelings were so confused, and I needed to get out of there, into the fresh air.

When I reached my friends, I could see they were in plain sight, no longer attempting to hide.

"Let's go," I said, walking in the direction we came.

"Annie, stop for a minute," said Millicent, grasping my hand from behind. "Are you all right?"

"I'm fine. I'm not sure what we're going to do about the book." I stared at the ground, unable to order my thoughts.

"I don't believe for a minute that you're fine," she persisted.

"Okay—I'll be fine," I said, about to continue when Alexandre cut me off.

"We need to get back. Annie, I'm sorry, but your quest for this book is at an end. I've heard of the Romanov monster. I'm certain she's much older than this man thinks. She will be no match for either of you. I'm not at all confident I could match her myself. I will certainly not risk Millicent in this."

"Alexandre, stop. I will help you, Annie. Whatever you decide."

"You absolutely will not. This marks the end of playtime. Millicent, we are going home now." Alexandre reached for her hand, and she continued to hold mine. She gave me one last squeeze before releasing my hand in favor of Alexandre's.

Alexandre said nothing as he pulled her after him. I followed along, knowing I must at least return to Boston to regroup. I felt hopeless. I couldn't take on a powerful vampire by myself. I wondered if Benjamin had taken precautions to warn the others. I was sure he had, but I decided to write him with this suggestion, anyway. At least this would give me something to do in the short term.

Then, there was Thayer. What I said in the tent was a lie. I wasn't using him for some dangerous fun. I had begun to fall for him. I could try to deny my feelings all I like, but it was true. There was something about him, something I felt from the first moment I saw him gazing at me through those half-closed eyes. I had no idea what was going to happen next, but I was sure it couldn't be good.

CHAPTER ELEVEN

Thayer

Misery had long been my friend. I didn't think I could live a more dreadful existence, but I was wrong. The pain I felt at betraying Annie's trust was like a thunderbolt to my heart. Surely, I was better off before she came into my life, but now she was in it, firmly. I knew now what I would do. I would betray Emilia. I had to.

Allowing her to destroy Annie was not an option. Emilia would punish me. How was the ultimate question. Would she snuff me out of existence like Captain Klein, not bothering to give me time to explain myself, or would she shackle me in a cold cellar for two hundred years? I wouldn't put an even crueler torment past her. If it meant Annie would be safe, Emilia could do whatever she liked. Without Annie in the world, my life meant nothing.

The woman had changed me utterly. Never had I cared for another living soul, mortal or immortal. Even wiping out Klein's camp would have left me feeling nothing. Before she came into my life, I only cared to do what Emilia bid. Her motto was *For the Family*. But what had the family ever done for me? They had never shown me love or warmth of any kind. I was a weapon and was always treated as such.

Annie brought out a tenderness in me I didn't know was there. Even if she meant what she said, I didn't care. I suspected she was untruthful, but no matter her feelings, I had not been toying with her. Once my mind was set, my resolve was like iron. I was sure I would be able to secure the book. Emilia trusted me, so gaining initial access would be easy. No one had ever betrayed her before. Why would she be suspicious?

Removing the book and then hiding its location would be more difficult. Emilia was as constrained by secrecy as any immortal. She could slaughter a handful of spies and wipe out her own camp of soldiers, but to unleash her wrath on a large group of people, not under her control, would shine an unwanted spotlight on her dealings. She would know I took the book, this seemed unavoidable. But perhaps I could keep its destination from her. Then, I would turn myself in. There would be no way around this—she would hunt for me for an eternity.

Any more thinking was pointless. It was time to act. I left immediately for the city, putting my second in command in charge, with orders to stay inactive until my return. I didn't expect to come back, but I couldn't very well tell my lieutenant this. The man was nervous to oversee the regiment but knew better than to ask me where I was going.

The bells from a cathedral were tolling midnight when I arrived in the city. The cobblestone sidewalks shone in the light of the moon, slick with intermittent rains. The rain left the city smelling fresher than usual, washing away the waste and grime for the time being.

I made my way to the expensive townhome, occupied by Emilia and her special guard. What I knew, which most didn't, was even more of this guard was housed in the two townhomes on either side of this one. Emilia never traveled without a full retinue. Why she felt she needed them didn't make a lot of sense to me. She rarely used this guard for anything, preferring to mete out punishments herself.

A block from my destination, I passed a small jewelry shop. Through the window, streaked with rainwater, was a ring glinting in the light of the streetlamp. The delicate piece of jewelry caught my eye. Ascertaining the street to be deserted, I forced the door of the establishment, closing it with a soft click behind me. I plucked the ring from its perch on the sill and placed it in my hand.

It was a gold posy ring, with a round-cut, aquamarine stone, shiny and clear. The inscription inside read *Always & Forever,* which seemed fitting. I slipped the ring in my breast pocket before dumping several coins on the counter, enough to cover the ring, and the door. This was not something I would have done before meeting Annie. I would have destroyed the door, stolen the ring, and never thought twice about it.

Feeling the small piece of jewelry close to my heart gave me a renewed sense of purpose. I never believed in what I fought for with my whole heart. I was an automaton, always doing as Emilia bid. Beliefs were not something I had the luxury of having. For the first time in forever, I felt something akin to conviction. This was the right thing to do. Annie not only thawed my cold heart, she had led me down a path of independence. That independence may lead to my sudden, painful death, but I felt free for the first time in my life.

I knocked on the door of the three-story, white-planked townhouse. I stood fully erect, like a good soldier, hands clasped behind my back. My mind had been shielded since leaving camp. I couldn't allow her even one glimpse into my thoughts. This would prove difficult, but if I failed, all would be for naught.

The door was opened by a footman. The man was small, with a blank face, his features unsophisticated. When one worked for Emilia, it was best to blend in, not be noticed. This man had perfected the dead-eye stare. Emilia employed a handful of human servants. These people were without families or friends. They knew if they ever spoke of what their mistress may be, they would not be missed.

I was admitted into the hall, where I was asked to wait. I was made to stand there for twenty minutes before being led into the bookless, soulless library at the back of the home.

The house was nothing more than a shell, which contained only the most necessary items. Its only purpose was to shelter Emilia while she was in the colonies. I thought its occupant fit in with her surroundings quite well. The home was devoid of any love or sentimentality, as was Emilia.

Emilia sat in a Queen Anne chair, her little feet propped on a velvet footstool. Dressed in her usual mourning black, she looked like a fragile doll. I could have laughed, as she was anything but fragile. She was the fiercest of devils.

"What brings you here, Thayer? Has something happened I should know about?"

"I have been thinking about the code book. I would like a chance to break it." I stood in the center of the room, my posture rigid.

Her eyes narrowed as she considered me. "This is unlike you. To leave your men and disobey orders. You know firsthand insubordination is something I cannot abide."

"Nothing is happening now. The men are fine. I only want to be as useful to you as I can. This book has stirred my curiosity. I have some experience breaking codes. All I ask is an hour or two with it. Then, I'll return to the camp. I'm confident I can do this for you." I kept my features stony while she regarded me for what seemed too long.

"I'm not pleased by this, but I'll agree. My codebreaker won't be here until tomorrow night. Maybe you can save me some time. It's on the desk." She waved vaguely toward the large oak desk behind her, returning her attention to the fireplace.

For this to work, I would have to feign a desire to work elsewhere. "I will need solitude, if you don't mind. I'll take the book to the parlor."

I waited for her to agree. After a few beats, she shrugged her shoulders. "As you wish. What an odd boy you are this evening."

I inclined my head, then retrieved the book. Measuring my steps, so as not to seem eager, I inched toward the door. As I moved down the hallway, I knew better than to rush.

"Oh, Thayer." Emilia's sharp voice behind me almost made me jump.

As it was, I managed to remain collected as I turned toward my mistress. Had I been found out? Had she managed to glean a disobedient thought from my mind?

"Be a good boy and keep the parlor door open. I want to keep one eye on that book."

I smiled. "Of course, Emilia."

I turned to the left, entering the parlor. I turned the pages as I sat. Leaving with the book in hand was proving to be as I thought; difficult. I felt foolish thinking I could walk out the door with such a valuable piece of property.

I gazed at the pages, waiting to hear her footsteps retreat to the library. I heard the creak of a floorboard. She was still standing in the hall. Was she suspicious of me or cautious about the book? She seemed to make up her mind, as I heard her footfalls walking back toward the library. If I breathed, I would have breathed a sigh of relief.

I pretended to study the contents for several more minutes before looking around. The door was out of the question. My eyes stopped on the window. It would have to be raised in absolute silence. I needed something to mask any sound I may make. I pulled the thick, red velvet rope for the butler.

When the sad Englishman arrived, I told him I wanted a fire made up. The hearth was opposite the window. While the man stooped, noisily adding logs to the mouth of the fireplace, I slipped the book into my coat.

Silently, I raised the windowpane and eased out, closing it after I was standing in the flowerbed outside. I hoped the man would either not notice my absence or not be bothered by it. Working for vampires, the human servant was used to odd occurrences. I wasted no time fleeing the city.

CHAPTER TWELVE

Annie

Fuming, I paced, making no effort toward silence as I slammed one foot, then the other down in rapid succession. There was no one to hear me, so I made the noise only for my benefit. Alexandre had taken Millicent to Savannah, Georgia. There was a home in the city he wished her to see. She was reluctant to leave without me but soon agreed after I made it clear I wanted to be alone. I wondered if I would always feel like a third wheel living with the two of them.

Alexandre made it obvious who his priority was. I almost felt sorry for the man. Millicent would tire of him, sooner rather than later. She stayed with him for ease, for comfort. Her time for blooming would come.

Upon returning, I dashed off a letter to Benjamin. I urged him to tell the others to flee. We were all compromised to a fatal degree. I wanted to become immortal to keep this sort of disaster from ever happening again. It seemed no matter how powerful I became, there would always be another who was more so. This was frustrating. I had a mad thought of rushing Emilia Romanov, grabbing the book, and setting it on fire before she could kill me. It would all be worth it, if only I could destroy those pages.

As I paced, a quiver went through me. I felt him. Thayer was here. Running to my window, I almost tripped over the braided rug. I tore open the shutters and pushed the window outward on its hinge. The night was windy. Fresh air hit me hard in the face. The branches from the oak tree creaked, swaying in the heavy gusts. Standing in the street, Thayer stared up at me. He held something in his hand. The Culper Code Book. It was a peace offering. I nodded my head, gesturing for him to come.

I moved to the Windsor chair next to the cold fireplace and willed myself to relax. He had brought me the book. Why? There could only be one reason. He cared for me. He cared for me above any concern he had for his own safety.

When the door opened, framing powerful Thayer in the light of the hallway, I jumped up and ran into his arms. He caught me, pulling me against his hard chest.

"What have you done?" I said into his neck, inhaling his scent.

"I would give my life for yours in an instant," he breathed into my ear.

"What do you mean, give your life?" Fear hit me cold in the face. I didn't like the sound of this.

"My life may be the price I am forced to pay for returning your book. But make no mistake, Annie, I would gladly do it again and again," he said against my hair, his arms tightening closer around me.

"Thank you is all I can think to say," I said. "You've saved more lives than just my own."

"I need you to do something, Annie. You must do a better job of shielding yourself. Your maker should have taught you this. I will teach you now. You must remain hidden from her, always."

"Is that how you found me?" I asked. Of course, Alexandre couldn't be bothered with teaching me actual skills.

"Yes, but I knew what I was looking for, which made it easier."

"Can you teach me later?" I asked as I began to kiss my way from his neck to his mouth.

Thayer said, "It should probably be now, but..." His sentence trailed off as our mouths met. His lips were soft yet firm. He picked me up in his arms, carrying me to the bed.

We were hungry for each other. Too hungry to take the time to remove our clothes. Thayer lay on top of me, propping up my right knee, before dipping his hand between my legs. His mouth was on my neck. I moaned, thrusting my hips toward him. He continued caressing me, bringing me right to the precipice of pleasure. Removing his hand, he freed himself from his breeches, then plunged inside of me. I called out Thayer's name in bliss, wrapping my legs around his. It wasn't long before we were both crying out in our ecstasy.

We lay for several minutes, entangled in each other's arms. Thayer nibbled on my chin, throat, and ears.

"Now, we do that again, but more slowly," he whispered in my ear, sending chills all through me. We removed our clothes, spending the next few hours devouring each other. Everything was so much more intense now with my vampiric senses.

When we were spent, I curled myself into a little ball by his side, my head on his chest.

"It's time for business. I cannot stay much longer, as much as I would like to," he said as he stroked my hair.

"Thayer, will she really kill you? I can't bear the thought. Why don't we run away?" I pressed myself up, so I could look him in the face.

"She will find me, eventually. She always will. I can only remain shielded from her for so long. And then, she will find you. This I cannot allow. She may not destroy me, but she will punish me. I have no delusions about this." I felt my stomach twist inside me. The thought of something horrible happening to Thayer left me in a near panic. I had never felt so connected to any man. Now, I was about to lose him.

"There's nothing we can do?" I asked, hoping for a miracle.

"I will try to lessen her anger. I don't want her to think anyone else is involved. My plan is to tell her I burned the book because I have lost my taste for back-alley killing. I will say it is dishonorable. Out-and-out fighting is the only way to battle with honor."

Emilia Romanov didn't seem like the type who would accept this sort of explanation, but I couldn't think of anything better for him to say. Over the course of the next half hour, Thayer taught me how to shield my mind from other vampires. He assaulted me with thoughts, while I tried to push him out, closing my mind. He was right, this seemed like something Alexandre should have taught me. It didn't take long for me to get it. When he was satisfied I had learned what I needed to, he left the bed to dress.

I sat up, pulling the blankets around me. "I hate that you have to leave. You're sure we can't run away?"

He pulled up his breeches, then sat on the bed next to me. "It would be my dearest wish—to run away with you." He leaned over, kissing me sweetly on the lips. "Keep practicing your shielding. It takes time to master control. Promise me."

"I promise." Of course, I would do as he asked. Emilia was not someone I wished to tangle with. "What will happen to the old couple in the woods?"

"They are well taken care of. No doubt they will be happy to never hear from me again. Don't worry about them."

Watching him dress felt like torture. Inside, my stomach hurt, and chest constricted. How could I let him go? I may never see him again.

He must have read this on my face because he said, "Don't worry. I am her family, after all. I have reason to believe she will be merciful."

"But, you said before, you would likely die for this." He was trying to appease me.

"I know. But the more I think on it, the more I'm sure she cannot destroy me. I'm too valuable to her. I will send word." He kissed me again, then finished dressing.

Standing before me, he brought his hand to the breast pocket of his jacket. "I almost forgot. I have something for you," he said, pulling out a ring.

Sinking down to his knees, he gestured for my hand. Unsure of which to give, I offered my left. It was closest, after all. Thayer took it, slipping a sweet posy ring onto my finger. The fit was perfect; as if it had been made for me. This was the first present I'd ever received from a man I had romantic feelings for.

"It's beautiful," I said, holding out my hand in admiration. I couldn't help but wish he would propose. Then I reminded myself that immortals probably didn't marry.

"There is an inscription inside, which sums up all I feel for you, Annie Monroe. Please don't read it until I leave." He stood in front of me until I nodded.

I was about to beg him to stay, when just like that, he was gone. Blood tears spilled down my cheeks. I fell over, burying my face in the blankets, heedless to the fact they would be ruined. I let myself sob. There had been many lovers, but no man ever touched my heart the way Thayer had. It was all too brief. If only I could see the future.

I now understood Millicent's melancholy mood swings. Wiping my face, I sat up. No matter what, I would not let anyone know my heart. This was for me, alone. I twisted the ring from my finger and read the inscription. Fresh tears fell from my eyes. *Always & Forever.* Yes, Thayer, I thought, I feel the same.

Thayer left the code book on the bedside table. Getting this to Benjamin at once was a priority, and it was imperative I pull myself together. I quickly dressed, concealing the book in my cloak. I knew where Benjamin resided in Boston but had never been there before. However, I couldn't trust this to a messenger. I had to do it myself.

Using my preternatural gifts, I was there almost immediately. Once I was standing in the alley behind his tasteful row home, I could feel my friend inside. Slinking like an alley cat, I made my way through the back door. There were signs of life in the kitchen; a half-empty tankard of ale, unwashed dishes piled next to the basin.

A gentle snore propelled me forward. I found the source of the noise in the office. The room was perfect for Benjamin. The walls were lined with long rows of books. Two expensive, brown leather sofas faced each other in the center of the room, placed over a perfect square carpet of navy blue. The well-used room emanated warmth and good taste. A fire had been recently lit. It was out now, but the room was still warm, smelling of wood smoke.

Benjamin lay sleeping, slumped in a heap over his enormous oak desk. The desk was situated so he could look at the garden beyond the window as he worked. He must have been exhausted. No doubt in great anxiety over the fate of the book, his network, and people. Benjamin's heart was a pure one. I left the book next to a stack of unopened letters with a note that read, *From your friend, Julia*. He would know what this meant.

Thayer

I left Annie as fast as I could. I couldn't bear to stay any longer. If I had, my iron resolve would have crumbled to dust. I knew I was in for a very difficult time with Emilia. Death seemed inevitable, but I couldn't let Annie be afraid for me. She would try to do something crazy to save me— this was her nature. The woman certainly had spirit, a spirit I lacked. Her aura was a fiery one, and she inspired me to be a better person. I was sure it was too late to begin living a good life, but I would go out doing the right thing.

Before leaving Boston, I decided to stop in some sleeping soul's home, borrowing some notepaper and ink. I entered the first house I came upon, making my way with surety to a desk in the parlor. There I found what I needed.

My dearest Annie. All is well, I have returned to New York and Emilia has forgiven me. I have been exiled and must return immediately to Germany. I dare not put you in danger by communicating with you. I will write only if I can. You must go on with your life. It will be a long time before we will see each other again. All my love, Thayer.

I sealed the letter, then slipped without noise from the house. I would post it tomorrow evening from New York, right before returning to face Emilia.

CHAPTER THIRTEEN

Annie

I may have been a tempest inside, but no one would ever know it. Wearing my heart on my sleeve was not me. I didn't see what good sharing my pain would do. Alexandre couldn't have cared less. He was terrified of Emilia Romanov and would not have helped had he wanted to. His only thoughts revolved constantly around Millicent. And that dear girl, sweet and caring as she was, was not in the emotional frame of mind to help anyone. I refused to burden her with my pain.

After Thayer left me, I fretted, pacing the length of my room so many times I could have walked to New York and back at least twice. I was sure I was wearing indentations into the wood of the floor. My fingers wound themselves through the ends of my hair, twisting and pulling until more threads than I cared to count lay along my path. I knew enough to realize I would be no help to Thayer. I would not be able to protect him from the Russian vampire queen. She was too strong. If anything, my rushing in would only put him in greater danger.

My only course of action in this case, seemed to be inaction. Not something I enjoyed. The morning was about to bring me the sweet bliss of black-out sleep, and I would be glad for it.

About thirty minutes before sunrise, there was a soft knock on the front door. I flew to the banister in time to see Alexandre accepting a letter from a messenger, a young, filthy child. He and Millicent had only just arrived back home, with Millicent leaving again as soon as she dropped her bags. Alexandre flipped a couple of gold coins into the waiting hand of the lad. It was nice to see him show kindness. The man still felt like a stranger to me.

I knew at this odd hour it could only be from Thayer or Benjamin. Alexandre closed the door, looked at the front of the letter, and then up at me.

"For our spy," he said, his mouth turned downward. "How much longer must this all go on? It's tiresome. You know, we will be leaving soon. Millicent will expect you to move with us."

I ran down the stairs as Alexandre spoke, snatched the letter, and yelled, "Thanks!" Then I ran back to my room. There was no time to address his selfish concerns.

As soon as I slammed the door shut behind me, I broke Benjamin's seal, an eagle, and unfolded the paper.

Thank the heavens for you, Annie. I've no idea how you managed to get the book, and I'm not going to ask. You have saved us all. Meet me at The Green Dragon tonight. I have a task for you. B.T.

A task meant a mission. A mission which would surely send me back in the field. I wasn't sure how I felt about this. Many of my jobs found me seducing men. With my heart now claimed, would I be able to sleep with another man? Would the pain I felt keep me from acting like an unconcerned maiden, or would it be etched on my face for all to see? How would Thayer feel about this? I imagined he wouldn't be thrilled. Yet, this was the commitment I made to the cause; to do what I must to aid in victory. I couldn't stop now, not when we were so close.

With dawn fast approaching, I didn't have the luxury of time to ponder these questions. My first course of action would be to find out what the job entailed, then go from there.

Before bed, I had some things I wanted to show Alexandre. The bottom drawer of my armoire contained the crucifix and holy water, given to me by Benjamin. I pulled open the drawer, digging them out of the back, where they'd landed after being tossed inside. These items were forgotten. Now, I couldn't wait to see what Alexandre would say about them.

Down in the parlor, I set the bottle of holy water on the small table next to Alexandre, draping the beads of the crucifix over the top, so the cross lay dramatically in front of its murky glass. I stood, watching my maker.

He glanced over, raising an eyebrow. "Why have you presented me with these trinkets? If you want to give me a present, Annie, I could give you some better ideas. I'm not really the religious sort."

"They're not presents. These are from a vampire slayer box. Have you ever heard of such an apparatus? Can these things hurt us? I assume not since I was able to pick up the crucifix without a problem." I sat down opposite Alexandre.

"You've answered your own question. This is a bunch of hogwash." As he said "this," he moved his hand over the religious paraphernalia next to him. "I've never heard of a slayer box but imagine it must be filled with more fancy. Killing an immortal is not so easy. This is amusing." He glanced at the items, picking up the bottle of holy water and sloshing the contents around.

I felt a little bad for my friend. Benjamin believed these trinkets, as Alexandre called them, offered him a measure of protection. They wouldn't help him at all. How could Benjamin and other humans like him protect themselves from the likes of Emilia Romanov?

"There were also silver bullets and pointy stakes of wood. Those are useless, as well?" I knew the answer, but still felt I should ask.

Alexandre barely looked at me as he returned to his book. "Nonsense," was all he said.

I wasn't quite finished with him yet. This was the first time I ever had Alexandre to myself. Not that I wanted him to myself, but I did have more questions. I was resolved he would at least hear me.

"A couple more things, Alexandre, then I'll leave you alone."

He sighed, looking me full in the face. "Promises, promises. Go on."

He regarded me over the edge of his book, not bothering to set it down. I didn't feel very high on Alexandre's list of priorities. For a moment, I sat contemplating this being I now called family. Why change me at all? Alexandre was clearly content, living away his days with Millicent. But she was not. She wanted me to join in their companionship, perhaps to act as a buffer between them. I could understand her reasoning, but not his. Millicent wanted a friend, a real friend. Alexandre merely wanted to make her happy. He was more of a conundrum to me than Thayer had been.

"What is your question, Annie?" Alexandre tapped his book on his knee.

"Why did you choose to come here?" I asked.

"To Boston?" Alexandre tried to clarify.

"More generally; to the colonies. It seems a strange time to begin a new life, with a war being fought around you."

He shrugged. "Maybe for mortals who have to worry about being caught in the crosshairs. Millicent and I needn't worry about such things. She needed a wholly fresh start, somewhere completely different. I couldn't get the Pacific between her and France fast enough. She wanted to visit Italy, but I knew I must get her farther away than that. After what happened, it was vital she start anew. What is a war to an immortal? This will all be over soon." He gestured in the air with his book. I thought this was the most I'd ever heard Alexandre say in one breath. Perhaps we could keep the momentum going.

"I know it will. The revolutionists are so close, we can taste it. This brings me to another question. Which side are you on, Alexandre? Mine or the English?" Millicent was fully on the side of the rebels, but Alexandre never made his fidelity clear.

"I'm usually on my side, my dear," he said with a smirk. "If pressed, I would choose your side, of course. However, it matters very little to me who wins and who loses. Nothing much will change for me, either way." He raised his eyebrows, then turned his attention back to his book. Existing on the fringe of society as they did, with powers which made them virtually untouchable, probably allowed Alexandre and others like him to feel like mere shadows. I still cared though, I always would.

"Is Italy where you're from, Alexandre?" He brought up an interesting thought when he said Millicent wanted to visit there.

Alexandre looked down at the carpet, then back at his book. "Where I'm from? Who knows. I can barely remember anymore. I try to live in the moment."

I suspected Italy was indeed where Alexandre originated. His profile looked almost identical to that of Julius Caesar I had once seen in a book. The light, almost curly hair, aquiline nose, and other strong features were so similar, they could be related. I remember thinking after I saw him for the first time in The Green Dragon, how he reminded me of that drawing.

"This must not be the first war you've ever been witness to. Which others have you seen?" I hoped to trick him into revealing some detail, but he was too smart for tricks and was clearly tired of my pestering.

"I told you, Annie. I can't remember anymore," he said, looking me full in the eyes with a hard stare before returning to his page. I was pushing my luck.

"Where's Millicent this evening? It's almost morning," I said, knowing this would annoy him. Why not push it a bit more?

"Clearing her head," he answered, not bothering to look up at me. People without conviction irritated me to no end. I suppose Alexandre was partially right, in that the outcome of this fight wouldn't affect him much. If Alexandre were human, I would say he looked tired, unwell. My guess was he was not happy. It was clear he adored Millicent. It was also clear while she depended on him, he was not the center of her universe. I knew how he wished he were.

"Okay, last question. Why were you so afraid of Emilia Romanov? Did you have a run-in with her?"

His eyes went hard, glassy. "I'm tiring of this game. If I answer this, you leave me in peace. I myself have never encountered the foul beast. Someone I knew, long ago, had what you call a run-in with her."

I nodded, urging him with wide open eyes to continue.

"Fine. I don't know the whole story. But this vampire was old, almost as ancient as Emilia, though I don't believe anyone knows her true origin. Anyway, this man tried to take over her territory in Russia. She not only annihilated him but also his entire preternatural family. There were at least eighty or ninety of them. Most of those people were not even involved or in Russia. She hunted them down one by one, taking them all out."

"My God," was all I could say.

"Exactly. Are we done?" He tapped his finger against the cover of his book.

"We are. Thank you for being willing to talk with me."

Alexandre made a mock salute with his hand as I rose to leave him. Emilia Romanov was one scary monster. Alexandre's fear made sense now. I learned all I could from Alexandre this night. I did think it odd when Millicent said she didn't know anything of his history. What did he have to hide? My instinct told me whatever it was, was probably huge.

The next evening I felt a strange unease. My mind was troubled, as if something had happened, something bad. My head throbbed with a phantom pain, my throat was dry, scratchy. I couldn't put my finger on what I was feeling. A queasiness upset my stomach. It was an almost nervous, unsettling shakiness. Was it Thayer? Would I know if the foul Romanov had hurt him? I wasn't sure. Thayer taught me to close my mind. He himself must have been skilled in this. He could keep me in the dark forever if he chose.

I rose from bed, needing to get dressed. Thayer was sure she wouldn't kill him, and I had to be too. My job was still foremost in my mind and must remain so until its completion.

My fine gowns had been delivered. Millicent spared no expense, but she was reserved in her choices. She knew me well enough to know I would prefer a simpler style than hers. I imagined her rifling through silks and velvets, very much in her element. I chose a pale-pink, silk polonaise with ruffles of white silk at the elbows and neckline. The underskirt was a cream satin embroidered with a floral pattern in the same cream-colored thread. Whilst securing a white bonnet under my chin, I slipped my feet into pink silk slippers. I never had owned a bonnet. My day-to-day headwear had previously been restricted to simple straw hats and caps.

I admired the ensemble in the floor-length mirror, turning all around as I did so. My friend had done well.

Speaking of Millicent, I could hear her below, arguing with Alexandre. As much as I wanted to talk with her, there would be time later. I avoided them by leaving out the back door. I knew Millicent would be curious about Thayer, but I couldn't bring myself to talk about it yet, if ever.

While I strolled to the tavern, past brick buildings and low hanging, wooden signs, I twisted the posy ring around my finger. If only I could look on this ring with joy. Instead,

I felt the tendrils of terror in my gut. I chewed on the inside of my lip. How long would it be before I knew his fate? I said a quick prayer, to no one in particular, unsure what sort of god cared about the likes of us. But I hoped, nonetheless.

Wiping any trace of worry from my face, I opened the door to the famous tavern. I was becoming more adept at hiding my feelings all the time. Thayer taught me many useful things. A blast of warm air hit me in the face, along with the mixed scent of close bodies, stews, and ales. The night was toasty. To step inside the sweltering room felt wrong somehow.

"Let's walk instead. It's Bedlam in there," said a clear voice behind me.

Feeling relieved, I closed the door, turning to face my friend and handler. "Thank goodness. It doesn't smell like a rose garden and gracious, it's so hot."

Benjamin laughed, taking my hands in his. He looked more like his old self. Concern still creased his handsome brow, but not as deeply as it had when I found him passed out over his desk.

"Speaking of roses, you look as lovely as said flower." He held out my hands to admire my gown, as I gave a swish of my hips.

"Do you like it? I borrowed it from a friend."

Benjamin narrowed his eyes. "Did you? Your business is your own, Annie. It always has been. My only concern is your safety. Are you safe?"

"I am. Perfectly safe. Don't you worry about me for one second." I gave his hands a firm squeeze.

He seemed convinced, releasing my left hand and draping my right over his arm. "Let's talk about what I have for you."

"Benjamin, I almost forgot! Thank you for the beautiful flag. It's a treasure and a most thoughtful gift. It will be dear to me always."

"I thought you would appreciate it, Annie. I also thought you would enjoy meeting Ms. Ross, which is why I asked her to deliver the flag herself."

"You were right. I'll never forget our brief meeting. Thank you for both gifts." I kissed his cheek. Benjamin blushed slightly, his smile widening further. How I loved my sweet friend.

We stepped off the sidewalk, heading for the park a block away. My stomach turned only once. This was a commitment. I must see it through, no matter what.

The night was a busy one, and we had to wait several moments for three carriages in a row to pass by. I was feeling anxious to hear what Benjamin had for me, and the waiting was becoming too much to bear.

"Tell me," I prompted.

Once we were alone, walking in the darkness of the park, Benjamin began. "It's dangerous. Deadly, even. I wouldn't send you if I didn't think you weren't the best person for the job. I'm almost hoping you'll say no."

"Go on." I kept my eyes on the dirt path, concentrating on Benjamin's words, not the pain in my heart.

"Benedict Arnold has come under suspicion. I believe he may be turning his coat, but need help finding evidence. His wife is rumored to be expecting. Knowing what we all do about Arnold and his character…"

"It's likely he will be looking for a mistress during this time." I finished for him.

"Quite." Benjamin paused. This sort of thing made Benjamin uncomfortable. I doubt he would ever dream of something as immoral as an affair. Asking me to be intimate with a man was never a request he made out-and-out—that would not be in his nature. "Benedict Arnold is a dangerous, unpredictable man. As much as I'm sure he would disagree, he is no gentleman. You would have to be careful with him, Annie. Maybe even more so than usual."

"True. But what I know about him would lead me to believe he is a man easily led, easily persuaded. His ridiculous arrogance allows him to believe he is above being tricked. This may be my way in. I could glean much from him, if only I appeal to his ego." We walked in silence for a few moments, both of us lost in our own thoughts.

"If anyone can do this, it's you, Annie. Still, your safety is paramount. You can refuse. I will not think less of you."

I pulled Benjamin to a stop, underneath the swaying branches of a maple tree. I took his hands as he held mine not long ago, meaning to put him at ease.

"I can do this. More importantly, I want to do this. This could be the last straw, the information which takes us over the finish line." I looked with resolution into Benjamin's eyes.

He nodded, sighed, and then said, "I know. Please protect yourself, at all costs. You mean more than anything else."

"I don't mean more than the cause, Benjamin. None of us do."

Benjamin wanted to walk me back home, "wherever that was." I kissed him on the cheek one more time, at the edge of the park, and said my goodbyes. It felt like a final farewell. My friend must have thought so, too. He scooped me into a firm hug before releasing me to pull out a packet of documents from his pocket. This packet contained everything I would need to become a new person in Philadelphia.

I walked home through the night, past peaceful homes and sweet-smelling trees. Back at the house, I held up my skirts, ready to ascend the front steps. Instead, I pressed my palm against my forehead as I leaned against the railing. What was happening with Thayer? How would I get word to him about this mission? This mission, which I knew would be my last.

"Excuse me, Miss." The small voice behind me startled me almost out of my skin.

I turned to see the same dirty, young messenger boy from last night, holding out a note. Reaching into my handbag, I grabbed hold of all the coins I had. I deposited these into the waiting hands of the lad. His eyes stared hungrily at the money, "Thank you!" he squealed, then ran down the road, skin showing through the holes in his shoes.

I knew the note was from Thayer without even looking at it. Sitting on the step, my mind reeling, I clasped the paper to my chest. Of course, I had to open it, but I was terrified. I ripped at the seal, devouring the contents. I closed my eyes. Tears threatened to fall, but I held them in check.

Exile. Exile wasn't so bad. I wondered how long a vampire's exile lasted. Surely, a long time. There would be no way to inform him about the job I was faced with. I would have to tell him after the fact. Millicent had said we no longer lived by any sort of moral code. I hoped this was true for Thayer, as well, and he would forgive me. If only I could talk to him before I left for Philadelphia. He had told me to go on with my life, to do what I must. What I must do was continue chipping away at the English.

Thayer

I steeled myself before announcing my presence. I raised my hand, knocking on the heavy black door. I could hear the echo of it on the other side and imagined Emilia, feet propped on her little stool, her ears perking up like a dog.

The sallow, drawn butler opened the door, admitting me to the house. Before the hunched man could ask me to wait, Emilia's cold, unearthly voice rang out. "Come, Thayer."

It was impossible to make out anything from her tone. She only had one. As soon as I entered her lifeless library, I knew I was doomed. Any thought of Emilia forgiving me flew out the window with the same thoughts of living happily ever after with Annie.

Two giant vampires stood like wooden soldiers, flanking the sides of the room between me and Emilia. She stood facing the fireplace.

"What should I do with you, my son?" Emilia asked, her back still to me.

I knew better than to answer, so I remained silent. I also knew begging or apologizing would do nothing to further my case. Best to wait for the hammer to fall.

Emilia turned, fixing me with her small, soulless eyes. "You've nothing to say for yourself?"

"No. I await your judgment."

Her eyes were beady, narrowed into slits. "I need to know why first. What was your motivation?"

"The answer is simple; the book had to be burned. I am a soldier. Sneaking, slithering, it is not honorable. Out-and-out fighting is the only righteous way to win a war."

"Your answer may be simple, but so are you. Slithering, sneakiness, as you call it, has won every war since the beginning of time. You have cost us a great deal. That book would have dealt a death blow on our enemy. For this betrayal, I will be forced to punish you, severely."

"I understand. Do what you must." I stood my ground. I expected her to fly at me, destroying me where I stood. Instead, she snapped her fingers. The two brutes moved to me, seizing my arms.

"Thayer, this will be your sentence. You will be bound by silver chains, sealed in a coffin, and buried beneath the ground. Only the people in this room will know your location. How long you remain there will be left to my whim."

I felt the first cold panic I had ever known. She meant to bury me alive. I wouldn't die; I would rot. The silver would burn and weaken me. I would not be able to free myself. This was worse than death. I had, in a way, been prepared for dying. But, to lie in a dark box, for who knew how long, starving, burning, it was more than my mind could process.

"Please, Emilia, have some mercy. Let me die with some honor."

Her face changed in a most revolting way; her eyes remained dead, cold, but her mouth turned up, ever so slightly, at the corners. I didn't think I could feel more afraid, but I was wrong. Her evil smile told me everything I needed to know; she could not be dissuaded. I would go in the box, buried beneath the earth. There was nothing I could do about it. I resisted the urge to fight. I would, at least, walk toward my destiny with my head held high. I thought of Annie, of why I betrayed Emilia, and it calmed me. She would be safe, and she would think well of me; this was all that mattered.

CHAPTER FOURTEEN

Annie, Two years later

Twenty-four months vanished in the blink of an eye. I never once heard from Thayer. The posy ring still sat on my finger, where he placed it all those months ago. When Benedict asked me about it, I said it was my mother's. An easy enough explanation, and one he accepted without reservation. He was far too conceited a man to believe there was ever anyone in my life before him.

I went to Philadelphia a few days after receiving Thayer's message. I ensconced myself there as a wealthy young woman from Boston. I became the belle of the balls, catching the eye of my target, Benedict Arnold. The man disgusted me down to my bones. He was a ghost of the handsome man he had once been rumored to be. His midsection was beginning to soften, and he limped around on a cane due to a grievous leg injury taken in battle.

But there was more to it than that. There was something hollow in his face, something dead behind his eyes. He was arrogant to a point that was loathsome, yes, but he also hated himself. His bearing carried a weariness, a sadness almost, when he would catch a glimpse of himself in a mirror. He went on because he had to, he had to prove to himself that he wasn't a piece of filth. I don't think he was ever convinced though.

One day, as we slept in Benedict's quarters at West Point, I dreamt of the dark place. I was reckless, staying with him in this way. But since we spent the evening before drinking, with Benedict passing out next to me, I didn't have much choice. The dream was so vivid, so frightening.

The darkness was thick, deep. Even with my preternatural eyes, I could see nothing, only a complete absence of color. I could feel a hysteria rising in my throat like a scream. I needed to move, to see. Only there was nowhere to go. Walls pressed in on me from all sides. Trying to move my arm, I felt a searing pain. Something heavy, so burning hot it was cold, pressed into my wrist. I felt the same burning across my chest, around my left thigh, and both ankles. I twisted my head from side to side, trying to move, trying to scream. The burning was so intense, it dulled my senses. I could feel the skin, burnt away, the metal now inflaming my muscles.

Benedict shook me awake. "Annie, wake up. You're having a nightmare."

His breath smelled of stale alcohol. I sat bolt upright, my throat and chest sore. I leaned back against the headboard. It was almost dark, and I could feel the sun setting. The images were from a dream, only a dream. How could pictures in my mind feel so real? I felt as if I'd been chained, buried alive. I couldn't think of where this scene would come from. Nightmares were unknown to me, and this one left me shaken.

"You were screaming. As if I don't already have a most wicked ache in my head." Thinking of himself, as usual.

"I'll get you some water." I moved to get out of bed when Benedict surprised me.

"I have nightmares," he said with the simplicity of a child.

"Do you?" I asked. "What are they about?"

"Battles, mostly. I hear men screaming as you just were. But, also…other things."

I remained unmoving, hoping he would elaborate.

"Yes," I prompted.

"The water," he said, shutting down the conversation for the time being.

Playing him was easy; there was really nothing to it. Benedict was at the end of his time in the colonies. It would soon be all over for him. One night, about three months into my time there, Benedict drank himself into a drunken stupor. He cried over his mistakes, telling me everything I needed to know, and then some. I was able to get the necessary information to Benjamin, thwarting Britain's plans to take West Point.

In the end, I almost felt pity for the pathetic man...almost. I considered draining him a time or two, but it seemed a more just fate to leave him as he was.

Now in our new home of Savannah, Georgia, I was determined to put my time in the revolution behind me. Alexandre and Millicent had fallen in love with this charming place. It suited Millicent to a tee; joyful and dark in equal measure.

The home Alexandre selected was a wonderful distraction for Millicent. She fussed, fretting over every single piece of furniture, every picture on the wall, every plant in the garden. I couldn't manage to drum up any interest in these things. My heart yearned for greater adventures. Two years in and she still hadn't finished.

This evening, Millicent pulled me along to the fabric shop. Most of the local stores were happy to stay open for her as she spent quite a lot of money. This evening, her sights were set on re-upholstering the chairs she chose for the library.

"You're not helping, Annie. Do you like the peach striped satin or the sky blue? I rather like this snow-white silk," she said in all seriousness. The shopkeeper buzzed around her, happy to be assisting such a well-to-do client.

I stood by the door, fingering velvets, eyeing the street outside. "You know I don't care. And we both know you don't care. You'll pick what you like, no matter what I say."

"Cheeky," she said, looking over her shoulder. "What's the matter with you? As Alexandre would say, you're pulling a Millicent." At least she owned her mood swings.

"I'm just so restless," I almost whined.

"Of course, you are. You're no homebody, Annie. You need the thrilling, the dangerous in your life. What you need is a new cause."

She was right. I did need a new cause. But what my friend didn't know was I needed a man, one man. Thayer Emmerich had disappeared in a puff of smoke. I considered traveling to Germany, to scour the country for him. But if he hadn't written by now, it stood to reason he didn't want me to go to him.

It was possible he heard about the affair with Arnold and was through with me. I looked down at the aquamarine posy ring while Millicent continued to chatter behind me. It felt suddenly like a vise, like something I couldn't escape from unless I cast it away. I wouldn't be like my friend. Although her circumstances were different, I wouldn't be tied down to a memory. Especially when said memory was of a man who didn't want me.

"I have to do something, I'll see you back at home," I called, not giving Millicent time to respond. The bell over the door clanged as I went out, and the cobblestones were slick from the day's rain. It felt good to be outside. The shop had begun to feel hot, oppressive.

I took off at a fast walk toward the riverfront, pulling at the ring as I went. I hadn't taken it off since the night Thayer gave it to me. I didn't think vampires gained weight or retained water, but somehow the ring had tightened. At one point, I was sure I would have to yank off my skin to pull the ring free. It wasn't until I reached the water's edge that it finally gave, slipping over my knuckle.

Holding the small piece of gold and stone in my hand, I considered it, turning it this way and that, to catch the light from the streetlamp. Then I read the inscription. My throat constricted unexpectedly. I felt moisture pool in my eyes. What did this one man have that no one else had? It was easy, if I were being honest. Thayer was brave, kind, strong, and had the sexiest bedroom eyes in existence.

I smiled. I did miss his eyes, his hands, and all the rest of him. He sacrificed everything for me. However, he had forgotten me. Even in exile, he should have been able to at least get word to me. I would have to move on, as well. I pulled back my arm, poised to hurl the simple ring into the fast-moving waters. But, I couldn't. My hand tightened around the ring until the gem cut into my flesh.

I had to keep it as a reminder. There would never be another time in history like this one; a time when the stars aligned and a people who should have easily, soundly, been beaten into submission, won. We won. The British House of Commons had informally recognized our independence. And as there would never be a moment in time like it, there would never be another man like Thayer.

I slipped the ring into my beaded handbag, turning toward home. When I got there, I ran straight up to my room and began emptying drawers and wardrobes.

"What on earth are you doing?" exclaimed Millicent behind me.

I turned toward my dear friend, opening my arms to her. "I have to go, my love," I whispered into her golden hair.

"Why?" She sounded like a child while grasping me tightly.

"You know why, you said it yourself. I need to find my new cause." She didn't say anything, didn't try to dissuade me.

We broke our embrace as she moved around me into the room. "When will you be back—do you think?" she asked as she began folding chemises.

"I'm not sure. But I'll be back. I'll send word when I'm settled, and you can come for a visit. You can stay as long as you like."

"Thank goodness. Alexandre is driving me insane."

Our laughter drew Alexandre to the doorway. "And what are you two up to?" he drawled. He had been trying out a southern accent. Millicent rolled her eyes; we laughed again.

Thayer

"Annie...Annie." I came to for another moment of tortured consciousness. If consciousness was what you could call this experience. There was a blackness surrounding me so deep, so devoid of any color, any light, I thought this was what death must be like. Except for the pain. I was sure there was no pain in death, simply a blissful unknowing.

I had no concept of time, no idea how long I had lain in this box. I was so delirious, so stupefied by the burning in my body, and the emptiness of my mind, I had forgotten long ago about the events that led up to this incarceration. The one thought which remained, the one word which seemed to mean anything, was a name. A simple name which brought me comfort.

Whenever I woke, I murmured the name, "Annie." It was a balm to me. Then, I would slip back into the darkness of my mind. This cycle was repeated many times. Losing consciousness was a blessing.

CHAPTER FIFTEEN

Annie, Present Day

Willing myself awake was difficult after a nightmare of the dark place. After two centuries of these dreams, I was no closer to understanding their meaning or origin. The images of the dark place were not common, but happened often enough, always leaving me shaken and confused. I was there in my mind, still, it felt so real, as if I were in the deep, inky blackness, feeling pain so intense I could think of little else.

"Do you ever have strange dreams? Dreams you can't connect to anything else?" I once asked Millicent after waking her with my screams.

"I have strange dreams all the time. But I know where they come from," she had answered. I wondered if I would ever figure this out.

I shook out my still sleepy limbs. Wretched did not begin to describe how I felt. Alexandre and I were not close, never had been, but to see the head of my maker severed from his body, kindled a deep sadness within me. Alexandre only ever had eyes for Mills. He was sick, yes, but his love for her ran deep. The man was also a lover, once or twice. Maybe more, it was hard to remember every moment of 240 years. He was many things to me over these centuries and now he was gone, never to return.

I had to pack up, had to get out of Savannah, again. The one other time I left for an extended period was after my affair with Benedict Arnold. Even then, I hadn't been gone long, the need to be with Mills pulling me back. Now the city held too many memories.

The events of the past few weeks awakened other recollections. Remembrances I thought were long dead and buried. A velvet pouch sat nestled into the bottom back corner of my jewelry box along with the crucifix given to me by Benjamin. The small Betsy Ross flag was displayed in a frame hanging over my dresser. The only other item I kept from those days was the exquisite Ottoman dagger.

I dug out the dagger and pulled it from its sheath, holding it in the air. The copper, now taking on a faded patina, still glowed in the light of the lamp. Perhaps it was the shine from my memories. Still, it was a beautiful sight. I thought of the press of Benjamin's fingers as he pushed the knife into my hands underneath the table in The Red Lion, all those years ago. These treasures would go with me, wherever I went.

I held the crucifix, rolling the beads between my fingers, remembering the last time I saw my dear friend. It was February of 1835, the day of his eighty-first birthday. I knew this would be our final meeting. The last time I saw him, before this, was at the park in Boston, where he tasked me with the mission of extracting information from Benedict Arnold. There was no way for me to explain my unaltered appearance, but it didn't seem to matter.

Benjamin was frail, unable to leave his bed when I arrived after dark. His second wife, Maria, admitted me to his room, then left us alone. I was almost overcome with emotion, seeing my friend, old and gray, propped up against a mountain of pillows, his head sagging forward.

His watery eyes, heavily lidded, but still bright, lit up

when he saw me. "Annie, are you an angel? Have you come to take me home?" His voice was raspy, quiet.

I held a bag of chocolate in one hand, fisting the other into the side of my dress as I stood in front of him. "No, Benjamin. I'm alive. The same as you, but different."

He continued to watch me, his expression one of wonder. I was unsure whether he would accuse me of vampirism and become upset, but he didn't. He only continued to look at me in awe.

"May I sit? I brought candy." I gestured to the chair next to his bed. Benjamin nodded.

Once seated, he reached for my hand. His skin, once so youthful and firm, was paper thin.

"Your hand is so cold," he said. "You look so lovely. You were always so lovely, Annie. So passionate." His voice broke, and a tear fell down his cheek.

"Don't cry, Benjamin. It's all right. I'm all right. Are you comfortable?" I asked, leaning toward him.

He shook his head. "Not really. My end is near, Annie."

I bowed my head over our clasped hands. It took all my power not to cry. I wouldn't scare my friend with tears of blood.

He patted my hand. "It's okay. I'm ready to go on. My life has been a happy one, a productive one. I've known love, fatherhood, and the love of my country. It's been a good life," he paused. "Has yours?"

"Yes, your life has been wonderful, Benjamin. A life of service is not always easy. You have so much to be proud of. My life has been good, too. I'll never forget you, my friend." My voice cracked, forcing me to bow my head once more.

"I'm surprised Maria allowed you in with sweets. What kind did you bring me?" he asked, bringing a smile to my face.

"You're favorite, of course, marron glace." I opened the bag, bringing forth a piece of the candy. Benjamin suddenly had the look of a child. It made me so happy to know I brought him a little joy at the end. I wept a great deal after leaving him that night. Benjamin died two weeks later. I would never know another person like him.

Taking a break from packing my clothes, I opened the box and pulled the velvet pouch from its resting place. There was no more avoiding it. I tipped the contents into my palm. The second the small ring contacted my flesh, my chest constricted. Why should I feel this way after such an expanse of time? The ring did not go back on my finger after almost being thrown into the water. Instead, it went into this box. I did not hold onto ghosts for an eternity.

No one could have predicted what happened to Millicent. To come face-to-face with a man who looked exactly like her dead lover, who in fact possessed the man's soul, was unbelievable. She was lucky. There was no way around it. Her love had come back from the grave.

I would have thought her delusional had Alexandre not confirmed the resemblance, then tried to kill the man to get him back out of his way. She was given a second chance with a man who died. The man I had loved was out in the world, at least, so I thought. I never once came upon him in all this time.

Granted, I never sought him out, nor had I ever stepped one foot in Germany. Perhaps he was still in exile there, playing fetch for Emilia Romanov. Emilia fell away with as much swiftness as Thayer had. All her scheming came to nothing in this country. How I would love to rub her nose in this fact. All her vindictive underhandedness did nothing but lead to the English being pushed out. I thought of her once, in the early 1900s. The brutal execution of the royal members of her family brought her back to my consciousness. I wondered how it happened, why she never intervened.

The thought of Germany remained in my mind. I had never been. It seemed like a beautiful place, with fairytale castles, and rolling countryside. I had to go somewhere, after all. Germany seemed as good a place as any. There would at least be cute boys and lots of good beer. Placing the ring back in its bag seemed cruel somehow.

An image of a close, musty place, thick with darkness assaulted my senses. I smelled earth, heard the crawling of bugs, felt a cold, clammy dampness. A tingling sensation, which grew into a feeling of white-hot pain, intruded upon all of this. I closed my eyes, shaking my head. Why did I keep feeling this place? Dreaming of it? Surely, I would remember had I ever been there. I chalked it up to the years, then slipped the ring on my finger. My breath caught, but only for a moment.

"All ready to go, rebel girl?" said Millicent, peeping over my shoulder.

"Just about." I tucked the pouch back into the jewelry box, then turned to hug Mills. We held on for as long as we could.

Alexandre's private plane sat at Savannah Hilton Head Airport. The plane was all comfort. It was Alexandre's pride and joy, one of them anyway. My limbs relaxed as I sank into one of the deep, cushioned leather seats, preparing to read the first of many steamy romances I brought along.

It was morning when we landed in Berlin, so I stayed onboard until the sun went down. The two pilots knew enough about us not to question. They were heavily compensated for their troubles.

Something strange happened when I woke. I was dreaming of the dark place. This itself wasn't unusual. What was unusual was the intensity of the dream. I had never felt it so strongly.

I sat up, feeling disoriented, clammy; almost gritty with dirt, though I was spotless and clean. I thought about calling Mills but didn't want to bother her. She was wrapping up the house in Savannah. When the plane returned to Georgia, she and Jack would take it to London.

This was a case of nerves. After what we had been through, it was no wonder. I couldn't get off the plane fast enough. Gathering my bags and walking to the door felt like walking out of prison after a ten-year stretch. Pausing on the bottom stair, I took a deep breath. I was sure the air outside the airfield would smell fresher. Now, all I was getting was fumes.

As soon as my foot hit the ground, I heard it, the faintest murmur, *Annie*. The whisper was so quiet, so momentary, I thought I must have imagined it. Just because a woman had always been strong of mind, didn't mean she couldn't slip, on occasion. I had been through a lot.

The whisper was familiar. Could Thayer know I was in Germany? If it was even him. He sounded terrible, frightening. Why would he sound that way?

A fresh thought dawned on me. I felt like the biggest fool who ever lived. I dropped my bag, doubling over on the pavement. How could I have been so stupid? Of course, she wouldn't send him into exile as his only punishment. She disciplined him much more severely. Still doubled over, I gripped my thighs.

My eyes found the ring, which now felt heavy, my veins throbbing beneath it. *Always & Forever.* You don't give a woman a ring inscribed with those words, then never contact her again. Unless you can't. Something has kept Thayer from reaching out all these years. Under his tutelage, I became adept at shielding my thoughts, keeping a barrier always around my mind. The only two I ever let in were Alexandre and Millicent.

Now, I let a portion of the barrier fall just enough to try to reach him. *Thayer, are you here?* I asked in my mind. *Where are you?*

A gasping sound reached me. It was inhuman, pained. Then another faint, *Annie*.

Standing straight, I tried to think. Where could she be holding him? Obviously, he was closer than he'd been in a long time. Then it hit me; the dark place. Thayer was in the dark place. I squeezed my eyes shut, blinking back tears. Now was not the time. I had to get to him; I could cry and feel guilty later.

"I'm coming, Thayer. I'm sorry it's taken me so long. Please hang on. Keep saying my name, if you can."

Mills had arranged a car for me. It was a small, compact thing which more closely resembled a clown car than an actual vehicle. Sliding into the driver's seat, I concentrated on Thayer. As I was trying to get the key to turn in the ignition, another faint gurgle of sound came through. It sounded like a place; a town, or perhaps the name of a castle. Whatever it was, it was Greek to me.

What was that? I asked.

There was no answer. He had slipped back into silence. I could figure it out, and my chief concern had more to do with what awaited me at this place. Would there be guards? I had no way to know until I arrived.

As I drove, the gasps and whispers became more distinct. When they faded, I knew I was heading the wrong way and would turn in the other direction.

Four stops and three hours later, I was pulling up to an old iron gate. The gate was twice my height, sturdy, and secured with the largest lock and chain I'd ever seen. Good thing I could hop right over this obstacle.

I pushed the car off the side of the road and hoped it was concealed enough by the brush and low-hanging trees. It was here I could feel Thayer. I wanted to vault over the gate, breaking into a reckless run toward the crumbling castle.

It was small, smaller than our home in Savannah. I called it a castle because it possessed some of the requisite elements; the gate, turrets, and even a lookout. The gray stone was old, medieval by my guess. It was clear this place was untended as weeds and wildflowers grew over the paths. Bits of stone lay in heaps around the perimeter of the building.

I checked myself. Reaching out ever so carefully, I felt one other being. Just one...this didn't seem right. It wouldn't be Emilia. I was sure this being was another lackey.

Buttoning up my thoughts so the vampire wouldn't feel

me approaching, I launched myself over the fence, landing in a crouch on the other side. All was quiet. With practiced stealth, I approached a small, wooden side door. It was locked. The urge to kick it open was strong, but I had to take the guard by surprise. I walked the perimeter of the stone building until I came to a cellar door. There was no lock.

I pulled the lid up with care, leaning it against the brick mouth of the cellar entrance, and glanced into the murky darkness below. There was no one, so in I went. Most of the ground was stone, except for a large rectangle, right in the center of the space. Running to the dirt, I began tearing into it with my hands. This was the dark place.

Over my head, I heard a creak in the floorboard. The guard must be dealt with first. I'll be right back, I thought.

I was not going to mess around. My mission was clear; kill what stood between me and my love. I crept my way up the stairs, pushing open the door. I found the guard in the dining room, of all places. A large jigsaw puzzle lay spread out on the huge ancient-looking table. The room was covered in a thick layer of dust, with big black spiders spinning their webs in every corner.

The guard's back was to me. In his ears were tiny earbuds. This was the best Emilia had to offer? She must have thought after this long, no one was coming for Thayer. She thought wrong.

I almost felt bad as I easily pulled the guard's back to me, breaking his neck. While he was stunned, I pushed the heavy table over, crushing his skull, puzzle pieces skittering across the floor. I couldn't take the chance of letting him live and I didn't have the time to sever his head.

I ran back down to the dirt patch beneath the castle, again digging into it with my hands. Before long, my bleeding knuckles hit something hard. It was a coffin. The bitch put him in a coffin. I hauled it up, onto the flagstones with my own two hands. Steeling myself, I pried open the lid and flung it back.

I sucked in breath I didn't have. If this was Thayer, I wouldn't have recognized him in a million years. He was worse than a decomposed corpse; he was a husk. Blood tears spilled from my eyes. Wherever tears hit, his wrecked body soaked them up. He was starved, with open wounds where the silver had bound him, burning his flesh down to the bone.

Searing my own hands, I pulled the bonds away, then flung them across the room. I picked Thayer up, cradling him in my arms. This man who had once been more powerful to me than a god was now pressed to me like a child. We left with a quickness, back the way I came.

I propped him in the backseat of the laughably small car the best I could. I needed some evil doers for their blood and I needed it now. Being out in the middle of nowhere, I couldn't find a single unclean soul.

I hated to do it, but I had to opt for a couple of large stags I could feel close by. Thayer was in desperate need of blood. Dragging the carcasses to the side of the car, I forced the nourishment down his throat. He was too weak to help himself. After draining the first animal, he was able to manage the other on his own. Thayer's skin cracked, creaking as he bent, almost making me sick to my stomach.

After he drained the animals, I drove us to a nearby inn, checking us in right before dawn. I secreted Thayer into the room—he still looked terrifying—then tucked him into the bed. We had yet to speak. I knew he would need time, and a lot more blood before he would be himself again. At least I hoped.

CHAPTER SIXTEEN

Annie

Thayer was gone. Instantly I felt panicked. This was a nightmare. I stumbled around the room as if I might find him under the bed or behind the shower curtain. He could have woken before me to feed, or he could have been snatched by the Romanov hag.

I had fallen into bed alongside Thayer fully clothed, so there was no need to waste time by dressing. At the same moment I was pulling the door open, Thayer was reaching for the knob, causing him to stumble right into me. He looked almost…normal. I breathed a sigh of relief.

"Thank the goddess," I said, relaxing my tense body. "Where were you?"

"I needed more sustenance." Of course, he did. I was glad he was able to get it on his own. I wanted to cover my ears, holding in the sound of his voice. To hear him speaking to me again, after so long, it was the most beautiful sound.

These were the first words we spoke to each other in 240 years. My head dropped a little, feeling the weight of this. Should we have said something more meaningful? What should those words have been? I backed up, allowing Thayer space to enter. He closed the door behind him, slumping against it. He may have looked more like the man I knew, but it would take a while to get his strength back. His eyes searched my face.

I shuffled my feet, unsure of where to go from here. I didn't know what he wanted. Did he want me as badly as I wanted him?

"I can't thank you enough for freeing me from my centuries-long torment, Annie. Much of the darkness is a blur now. A painful, confusing blur." He paused, looking into the distance. "But, Emilia is still out there. She will find us, she will kill us."

Before I could respond, he added, "The horseless carriages are quite something, aren't they? Not to mention these lights." His hand wandered to the light switch, then flicked it up and down with his index finger.

"There will be a lot for you to get used to, to learn. You won't believe all that has changed." I sat on the edge of the bed. "Do you think she still exists? Or that, if she does, she still cares that much? You were not well-guarded, and well, it has been a long time."

"She still exists. If she were gone, I would know. I wounded her pride, all those years ago. This is enough to keep her on my heels. She could be more dangerous to me now, and to you."

I went over in my mind what I had been through with Alexandre. A shudder went through me. He easily bested me, tossing me through the air as if I were nothing but a rag doll. If memory served, Alexandre was afraid of Emilia. Alexandre, the man who would have ended me had it not been for Millicent and Jack, working together. If Alexandre was afraid of Emilia, maybe all she would have to do is snap her fingers and I'd fall dead. Not a pleasant thought.

The situation seemed impossible. This was a time when one must weigh everything. Yes, there was a possibility of death. But, dying was better than continuing to live without

Thayer.

"You can't possibly want to go back into the abyss," I started. "And…I would rather die than live another 200 years without you."

He looked at me from the door. Those sleepy eyes which always hovered on the edge of my unconscious mind fixed me in their gaze. He walked toward me, then scooped me up in his arms. Crushing me to him, he buried his face in my neck. I held on for dear life.

"Rosewater. How I've missed this scent. Thank you for not changing too much, Annie. We're going to die, you know that," he whispered against my flesh, sending chills through my limbs.

I thought of Millicent and Jack, a frail human. They defeated Alexandre with little help from me.

"Maybe," I said. "Maybe not. Either way, we do it together. You are not going back into that hole and I am not going on without you."

Our lips found each other. I could have cried again. Nothing felt as right as this. Nothing. Thayer grasped the back of my neck. Bringing my head back, he kissed his way down my throat, then brushed his lips along my clavicle. I thrilled in his embrace.

Clothes came off with ease. We would have time for play later. Right now, I needed him inside of me, his delicious weight on top of me. No one felt the way Thayer did. He kissed me sweetly as he made love to me. He seemed to come more alive with every moment. I turned around, changing position, his breath hot on my neck. Funny how we continued to breathe, around only each other. Habits were hard to break.

After, he lay spooned up behind me, tucking me as close to his body as possible. Thayer nibbled on the back of my shoulder, reigniting my passion for him.

"I hate to break the spell, Annie. But we should plan our attack. We don't want to leave anything to chance with her." Spoken like a true soldier, one with a price on his head.

I hated to agree, but I did. The need to end Emilia Romanov was at war with the need to remain cuddled up to Thayer.

"Any ideas?" I asked. I was sure he would have one or two. He knew her the best.

"We have to isolate her somehow. And, it won't be pleasant, but I think immolation should be our goal."

I grimaced. "You want to set her on fire?"

"I know, it will be unpleasant. But it may be the best way to destroy her without getting too close. If she gets close enough to get her hands on us, we're through."

He was right, Emilia could crush us. Still, the thought of burning someone alive was disturbing. Even if that person was as vile as our villain.

"By isolating her we can reduce the collateral damage. If my instincts are correct, once she's gone, our problem will be at an end. If I know any of those who remain under her, they loathe her as much as we do. Fear of her is what keeps them in check."

The question was how to lure her out. The other was; where was she? I asked Thayer.

"I doubt she has changed her headquarters. She will be in St. Petersburg."

Cool, I thought, another place I've never been that I won't be able to enjoy. I didn't share my sarcasm with Thayer. Millicent would have enjoyed my cheek, but Thayer wouldn't get it. He was still of another time.

"Are you sure about that? You don't know what happened in 1918," I said.

"What do you mean?"

"The Romanovs, the entire royal family, they were executed when the communists took over Russia."

"My, God. All of them?" he asked.

"Yes. All the mortals. I've no idea what happened to Emilia or her kind after that."

"What are communists?"

"Communism is a nineteenth-century thing. Something

I can explain later. They are no longer in power there. Perhaps, Emilia returned after their fall. It's the best place to start, in any case."

In the end, we decided to create a distraction a couple of miles from her fortress. When she sent her minions out to investigate, we would move in.

"It sounds simple enough, but I think we would have a greater likelihood for success with more help. If there's one thing I learned from spying, it's always helpful to have a man on the inside." I turned toward Thayer, propping my head on my elbow.

He turned on his back, staring up at the ceiling. "Yes...you may be right." He paused. I could see him chewing the inside of his cheek. "There is someone. But it's been so long, and it sounds as if so much has happened since I've been gone. I'm not sure if she would help us."

"She?" I asked, hoping he wouldn't hear the jealousy I was sure had crept into my voice.

"She and I were close, before the war," he said, tapping his fingers on his chest, deep in thought.

Of course, I had no right to be envious. I hadn't spent the last centuries in a convent, while poor Thayer had spent the years in a device of torture. And he knew this woman before me. I was being irrational.

"All right," I said, making up my mind. "Where do we find her?"

"She should be right here. Close by, at least."

"Are you sure? Don't forget how long it's been."

"We are creatures of habit, Annie. Where have you been all this time? Moving around?" He had a point. I hadn't moved my home base of Savannah, until recently. Yes, I left from time to time, but I kept returning. Always because Mills was there, but still.

"All right, as soon as night falls, let's find her," I said, resting my head on his chest.

Berlin wasn't far, and we were there in less than an hour. It took less time with Thayer guiding the way. I still felt strange driving such a small car, but managed.

Thayer was like a child during the drive; marveling at everything. One hand trailed out the window while the other played with every dial and button on the dashboard.

In Berlin, we pulled up to a very pretty home. Mills would have loved it, being a connoisseur of such things. The stone house was a soft, muted green with white trim around the windows and doors. The home had a fairytale-cottage look which fit with its location on the outskirts of the city. Had I seen a line of gnomes marching in the front garden, I would not have been surprised. Walking up the front path, I didn't take Thayer's hand. I wanted this woman to help us. If that meant creating some distance between us, then so be it.

When I mentioned this to Thayer, I could have sworn he almost smiled. "I will not manipulate her."

I said, "A little manipulation can go a long way in helping us with this impossible task."

Thayer pressed the bell. The second loveliest woman I had ever seen answered the door. I felt the green-eyed monster of envy worm its way into my chest. She was tall, lithe, with a delicate face. Light-brown hair fell past her shoulders in waves. She was an elf, living in a gingerbread house. Her blue eyes betrayed nothing. If she felt anything at seeing Thayer, she didn't show it.

"Ingrid," he said quietly.

"Thayer," her voice was sweet with a lilting cadence despite her heavy accent.

"May we speak English for the benefit of my friend? This is Annie." Thayer motioned toward me.

She turned a fraction of a degree, extending her hand with a slight smile. "Thayer doesn't make friends easily. You must be special."

I returned her grin, shaking her hand. "It's nice to meet you, Ingrid."

"Well, come in. You must be here about something important. I never have guests and don't want to set the neighbors to talking."

She widened the door, standing back for us to enter. When we were situated in the elegant front room, all creams, yellows, and greens, Thayer began. "Where is she, Ingrid? Still in St. Petersburg?"

"She is. First, tell me how you escaped. Did you rescue him, Annie?"

Ingrid looked at me, but it was Thayer who spoke. "She did. Annie and I met during the last war. The last war I fought in, that is."

Ingrid nodded. I decided to drop any pretense. We needed to move quickly. This was a woman who would appreciate directness. Thayer trusted her, or we wouldn't be here.

"She'll come for him again," I said. "We can't let that happen. He's spent enough time bound and buried in a coffin. Thayer and I have a plan. But we could really use another pair of hands."

Thayer turned toward me, his eyes wide. This was not how this was supposed to go. In fact, I wasn't planning on talking. He wanted to finesse the situation, work our way up to the battle. Ingrid would not have responded to any tactic. I could read that from her almost immediately. This was a woman who would respect directness and respond to it. I did have some expertise in this area.

Her eyebrows went up, but her mouth remained a straight line. She seemed intrigued but understood the seriousness of what I was proposing. She rose and clasped her hands behind her back as she took a turn around the room. Thayer and I remained silent, letting her think.

She came to a stop in front of us. "I hope you have a solid plan," she said, looking from me to Thayer.

"We do," he assured her.

"Let me hear it," she said, resuming her seat.

CHAPTER SEVENTEEN

Annie

"I think we're all likely to die," Ingrid said after we laid out the plan for her.

"You'll be the safest," I said. "All we need from you is to set off the distraction, then you can leave. Thayer and I are the only two who are risking our lives. But what little chance we do have, would be nothing without you." Our plan was a straightforward one. I often found the simpler plans had the greater chance of success.

Ingrid would set off a series of three small explosions, far enough away from Emilia's home to draw out what we hoped would be most of her henchmen. According to Ingrid, Emilia still ruled with an iron fist, but rarely left her home. Rumors were circling the family that she may be cracking under the strain of the years.

Very few family members had seen her since the infamous execution of the Romanovs in 1918.

"I believe it broke her, Thayer," said Ingrid, a forlorn look on her face. "You will not have heard of it, but this execution was vile, heartless. The loss of the royal family, the family Emilia watched over as a strange sort of guardian angel. It was too much. She wanted to keep the remaining Romanovs intact, but even this grew to be a burden for her troubled mind. She rules, but there is less to rule now. The world is so changed since you were punished. I still hear from time to time, of some sentence Emilia has brought forth on one of our kind. But there's no rhyme or reason to it. An organic brain, it is meant to live for only so long. We will all face madness eventually."

"She was always mad," said Thayer.

"Not mad. Ruthless, calculating, but not mad. I fear she is more of a danger now than ever. There will be no reasoning with her."

"There never was," said Thayer, staring into the distance.

"Why did she not help them?" I asked Ingrid.

"She tried. It was rumored Emilia had spirited away one of the little duchesses, possibly more than one. I have no idea if she succeeded or not. I'm sure you heard of the various individuals, several years after the fact, who claimed to be children of the Tsar and Tsarina. It's possible one or two of them went on. I certainly hope they did. Emilia always tried to keep her machinations under cover, not wishing to expose all the members of the family. She has never explained herself to me, so this is only conjecture. And, I haven't seen her with my own eyes since right before that horrible time."

There wasn't much else to say, so we continued with our plans. Emilia's home was isolated; we wouldn't have to worry about innocent bystanders or drawing human police. Thayer and I would lie in wait. Once we saw the house emptying, we would move inside, taking care of the remaining guards. In an ideal world, we wouldn't have to ever deal with Emilia. But the more we discussed this, the less we could see any way around confronting her.

Thayer would incapacitate her, while I started the fire. I squirmed in my seat. I hated the idea of the fire, and I was unsure about Thayer's ability to take out such a powerful monster. Ingrid sensed my discomfort.

She looked at me, saying, "She won't suffer long, Annie. Fire burns us with more intensity than a human being."

Her words only served to add to my growing nausea.

"I've done horrible things, Annie. This would pale in comparison. You must know this," Thayer said to me.

"It might not be the best plan, anyway," continued Ingrid. "It will take too long. We must strike her faster. Destroying her brain will be more efficient."

I felt this may be more difficult for me than anything else. But fire—fire seemed needlessly cruel. "Ingrid's right," I said. "It will cost us too much time."

"And," Ingrid interrupted. "You'll need my help, Thayer. No offense to Annie, but I can sense her youth. The two of us are older, more capable of facing Emilia. I'm tired of her inconsistent, harsh rule. It's time she goes. Ending her is the merciful thing to do."

I wasn't about to be left out of the fight, but she was right. "I can set off the explosions. Then, I'll circle back to join the two of you. The more hands, the better."

In the end, this was the course of action we agreed to. We stayed the day with Ingrid. She never said a word about our relationship. She only showed us to a room; a room we would share. Then, she left us.

I was a little antsy. "You're sure we can trust her?"

"We can. I saved her life, long ago. She always said she owed me." Thayer lowered himself on the bed.

"This is a big payment. What did you do?" I asked, sitting next to him.

"Ingrid loved a young, human man. This was in the late 1600s. Emilia found out, forbidding the relationship. Ingrid continued. One night, Emilia took them both. She stood the man in front of Ingrid, slitting his throat. She collected his blood in a chalice, then passed the chalice around the room. All the while, Ingrid screamed, trying to break free. I held her back. She was my closest childhood friend, the one person from my human life who followed me into immortality. Emilia would have destroyed her, had I let her go. As it was, I talked Emilia into letting Ingrid live."

"I hate her. I hate Emilia Romanov." I sucked on my lip. I detested needing to ask but couldn't help myself. "So, you and Ingrid were...friends, not?"

Thayer laughed. "Not everyone is a lover, Annie."

"I suppose not, but they can make life more fun," I teased, pulling him to me. "We may as well make the most of the remainder of this night."

Close to dawn, I left our room to sit outside on the front porch. Thayer was fast asleep, but I knew my mind would reel until I blacked out. I still had about thirty minutes and thought a breath of fresh air would help, as it usually did.

I took a wicker chair on the porch, looking up and down the small, residential street. Not a soul was out, but me. The near morning air was chilled in a way that didn't feel cold but instead felt bracing, exhilarating. A lone tabby cat meowed from under our car. I wondered if she had a home, then thought about bringing her inside.

"If you're wondering about the cat, she belongs to my neighbor. There is a pet door, so she can go in whenever she wants," said Ingrid as she closed the rounded, white door behind her.

"She wants to lurk. Who can blame her?" I asked, trying to lighten the tension between us.

Ingrid laughed, softly. "Exactly. We know all about lurking."

"I want to really thank you for helping us, Ingrid. You don't know me from Eve. What you've agreed to do is very generous."

"I may not know you, but I know Thayer. He is a hard man but has always had a gentleness inside. Of course, he would deny that. Still, it was always there." She paused. "He saved me, you know."

"Yes, he told me. I'm so sorry. My friend also lost the love of her life once. I can see why you want Emilia's reign to come to an end. She is a foul, unfeeling thing," I said, looking down at my hands.

"All we can do tomorrow is our best. Working together, hopefully it will be enough," she answered.

We said good morning, parting as friends. I couldn't help but look back for the tabby. She was gone. I hoped safe in her home.

My neck was tight with tension. Stretching it out did me no good. Far from relaxed, I dressed as tactically, as I could—black pants, black boots, black sweater. My hair was pulled back into an unforgiving, tight ponytail. I couldn't have the distraction of it falling in my face. My companions all had the same idea, each of them looking like hired hitmen.

We went into the night, looking like trouble to passersby. Not only because of our clothing but the weapons Thayer and Ingrid held in their hands. Ingrid carried a sledgehammer. Thayer had an old sword.

Last night, Ingrid removed the rusty weapon from over the fireplace. It had belonged to her lover, the one item she had as a remembrance. Thayer worked the piece of steel until it shined, bringing it to a lethal sharpness. I too had a weapon. Tucked into the back of my pants was the Ottoman dagger gifted to me by my long-lost friend, Benjamin Tallmadge.

Words were few and far between. The plan was set, and there was no need for chit-chat. Berlin was a bustling city, full of brick and skyscrapers. Old world meets new. We took to the tops of trees and buildings to expedite our journey out of town. We kept to less populated areas, never stopping for a moment. The trip which would have taken at least twenty hours by car took us about five on foot. We would not have much time once we arrived. Finding shelter for the day would prove difficult, but it was a risk worth taking.

Emilia's palatial home was a good clip outside of the city. Isolated, yet close enough to St. Petersburg to keep her comfortable, I supposed. We did a quick reconnaissance of her residence before setting the explosions. The once spectacular place reminded me of Varykino from *Dr. Zhivago*. I imagined it was stunning in its heyday. The large building was topped by golden domes with spires reaching to the sky. The gold had dulled over the ages, but I could see what it had once been before the communists took hold in this country. The home would have been opulent, fit for a queen.

After what seemed like forever, we were at the agreed upon location of explosion number one. Thayer went to work, setting up the three devices pilfered from a police station at appropriate intervals. Then he handed me the detonator he wired to control all three bombs. For someone so out of date, he was a quick study, thanks to the information we found online. I would hide a distance away, detonating one bomb at a time, watching to make sure our distraction was a successful one.

Then, I would join Thayer and Ingrid inside the house. Here I was, preparing for my second battle in two weeks. It was surreal. If someone told me a month ago what the near future held, I would have laughed until my sides split.

When Thayer was certain I knew how to handle the detonator, he kissed me on the cheek and walked off. We were both at a loss for words. Even if we knew what to say, there wasn't time. I shook hands with Ingrid, then she followed him into the night.

I took deep breaths, even though they did me no good. Crouching behind an ancient tree, I tried to get as comfortable as possible. I looked at my watch. I was supposed to give them precisely four minutes, then blow the first device. Those four minutes seemed to drag on like an endless school day.

Finally, it was time. I pushed the first without hesitation. A brilliant explosion went off, just as it should have. A loud boom sounded, followed by a veritable firework show of bright white sparks. The echo resonated through the forest.

I heard them almost as soon as the boom sounded. Her soldiers were coming. Time for the second blast. That one also went off without a hitch. Shouted commands echoed through the night, along with the pounding of more running feet. Still, I didn't think it sounded like a lot of soldiers.

I pushed the last button. Nothing happened. I pushed it again, fretting over what to do. Then, I threw down my device, running after Thayer and Ingrid. There was nothing to be done about it. All I could hope for was the two explosions had drawn enough men from around Emilia.

I was to meet up with my fellow assassins in the second-floor hallway, keeping my mind concealed. I entered the house through the wide-open front door. Everything was dark. What I could make out was old, tattered. I was disappointed. This amazing space had gone to rot. Dust was piled on almost every surface. Spider webs hung in every corner. It seemed odd but in keeping with what Ingrid had said. Were these the surroundings of a woman whose hold on reality had begun to slip? Why hadn't her people bothered to keep the home tidy? Perhaps they no longer cared, or perhaps, without explicit orders from their master, they were lost.

The house was still. I went to the stairs. There was the crumpled body of a soldier on the landing. But he was the only one. It seemed her ranks had slipped over the years along with her mind. I started to think we may prevail.

Thayer and Ingrid were positioned outside a pair of double doors. This must be the entrance to her lair. Once I joined them, Thayer bowed his head for a moment, then turned the knob. Time seemed to slow down. I could hear nothing; not the creaking of a floorboard, or the ticking of a clock. We seemed to be standing in a void.

The door swung open without a sound. She was lying on the bed, her back to us. She was small, almost as small as a child, I thought. The bare mattress she lay on was soiled, stained a deep russet color I assumed to be blood. The gown she wore would have been appropriate for 1776 and was no more than a rag. Still, it was her size, which astounded me. It seemed impossible to my mind that this tiny being could hold such malevolence within her.

Thayer and Ingrid didn't move. The weapons they held hung loosely in their hands. They were supposed to be moving, and with haste. Tension rooted in my neck, sprouting through my limbs. What were they doing? I reached out, touching Thayer's arm with my fingertips. His head spun, his eyes were wide with terror.

His terror ignited mine, although I didn't understand it. Why should he be so afraid? Could he not see her with the same eyes I did? Then, a voice, small, cold, inhuman, reached my ears. It made me shudder down to my boots. We all shook with a force that would have broken the bones of any human.

Thayer's head snapped back to the figure on the bed as it said, "Come home, have you? How lovely. And you've brought playmates." She never stirred. It didn't seem possible the words had come from the creature on the bed.

A chill crept its way down my spine. Sweat was gathering at my lower back and under my arms. Vampires didn't sweat. This creature inspired an almost primal fear. She hadn't even moved, until she did. Quick as a flash, more quickly than I'd ever seen anything move, she was off the bed. I couldn't register where she had gone for a second. Faster than being struck by lightning, I felt something hit me hard in the chest.

I flew backward, hitting the wall on the other side of the hall and crashing through it. Not again, I thought, as I fought against chunks of broken plaster and furniture to stand. Internal blood, likely from my lungs, poured from my mouth. I spit out as much as I could, then ran back to the mouth of hell, intense pain racking my breastbone.

Thayer and Emilia were locked in arm-to-arm combat, Ingrid stood poised with her sledgehammer raised over her head. There was no getting a good shot. Thayer's sword lay by the door. I had no idea what to do. Emilia and Thayer moved, hitting each other so fast, there was no jumping into the fray. Emilia kicked Thayer in the stomach, sending him crashing out the second-story window.

"No!" I cried. The creature laughed maniacally, then went for Ingrid.

Emilia sped around, grabbing Ingrid from behind and pushed her to her knees. Emilia's movements were so impossible, so rapid; how could we defend? Ingrid dropped the sledgehammer close to my foot right before her eyes met mine. They were calm, steady. Emilia had her hands, the size of a doll's, around Ingrid's throat.

"Take care of him, Annie," she whispered, right before Emilia twisted Ingrid's beautiful head from her body and stomped through her skull with a bare foot.

I know I screamed. My face felt wet, but I would not let this evil bitch win. I lunged for the sledgehammer, swinging with all I had. She caught it in her hand, her face tilted, her dead eyes focused on my throat. I tried to pull it free, but it was no use. I had given Emilia my best shot and it was nothing to her.

"You're the one, aren't you?" she said, so softly I could barely hear her. Her voice would give me fresh nightmares for decades. "You're the one he gave the book to. I always thought he gave it to someone. Thayer, always so clever."

Her beady black eyes made their way from my throat to my eyes. I wanted to scream again, afraid she could mesmerize me or transfer pieces of her evil soul to mine. My body was clammy; cold, but sweaty at the same time. Before the scream could escape my lips, Thayer was there, in the corner of my eye. I saw a flash of metal, then felt Emilia slacken her hold on my weapon. Thayer had used the Ottoman dagger to sever her arm. It must have fallen from the waistband of my pants as I flew. Then, there was a scream, but it wasn't mine.

While Emilia clutched at her bleeding stump, I swung the sledgehammer again. This time I contacted her skull. There was a wet, cracking sound which under normal circumstances would have sickened me. In this case, it was a delight to my ears. She slumped to the ground. I continued to pound until Thayer grabbed my arm, saying, "That's enough."

CHAPTER EIGHTEEN

Annie

The floor was hard beneath me as I collapsed onto my backside. There was a sort of sweet justice in the fact Benjamin's dagger had dealt the decisive blow which changed our momentum. To say I was stunned would be an understatement. Another victory that didn't feel like victory. Yes, we defeated the evil queen. I delivered the death blows, rather than lying unconscious under a tree. But we lost Ingrid. I'd known her all of twenty-four hours.

Her bearing and manner reminded me so of my beloved Mills. I was sure I would have befriended this woman, given the time. As it was, she lost her life helping to free Thayer. I could do nothing but watch as Thayer pulled a blanket from the bed, wrapping the body and ruined head of his friend.

Talking while he worked, he said, "I won't leave her here, but we have to move. We'll be set upon in no time."

I could hear them, too. The soldiers were rushing back to the house. Although, if I was being honest, it didn't seem as if they were running too fast. I snapped myself from my reverie, helping Thayer in his task. Of course, we wouldn't leave Ingrid.

"Follow me," he said, scooping his friend into his arms.

Instead of going down, he went up, with me at his heels. An attic window was half open. This seemed in keeping with the condition of the rest of the house; uncared for. Thayer pushed it the rest of the way as he stepped out with Ingrid. We danced along the treetops before dropping next to a car parked along the deserted road.

We spent the day at a small inn outside St. Petersburg; Ingrid safely out of sight in the trunk of our stolen car. I couldn't help but think how I would have loved to explore this historic city. Pleasure traveling would have to wait for another time.

"What will we do with her?" I asked once we were alone in our room.

"I will bury her next to her sweetheart outside Berlin. It's what she asked me to do."

"Last night?"

Thayer nodded, his eyes on the floor. "Right after we left you, she made me promise to do it, should anything go wrong."

"Almost as if she knew." I brought my hands together in my lap.

"Almost. She was ready."

"Do you think we have to worry about any retribution?" I was afraid of the answer but would rather know what we were in for.

"I don't think so. In my time, Emilia's home was the center of a hundred warriors, at least. I counted less than thirty. The house was in terrible disrepair, the attic window wide open. Emilia was not in her right mind. Her rule had become a broken one. My guess is her few remaining followers will be happy to be rid of her; free to finally live their own lives."

I had thought the same thing about the house. She was

dangerously mad, and it was good riddance.

"Where does this leave us, Annie? You have lived in the world these last two centuries. Is there someone else in your life?" Thayer looked me in the eye. He was serious.

I would have thought our first night together would have assured him of all this. His sexy eyes made my skin tingle.

"There is only you. Ever since you left, for what I thought was exile, there was always this block inside me, allowing me to only feel a little. I never let my emotions go further. It's been torture, actual torture for you. But all this has brought us to where we are now, sitting in front of each other. This is it this time. I can see your heart, Thayer, your kindness. It shines through your eyes."

"Are you asking or telling, Miss Spy?" he asked, the corner of his mouth twitching upward.

"I'm telling," I said right before pulling him to his feet.

Moments before dawn, we lay in a heap on the thick, warm hearth rug. "Do you remember the first day we spent together, in your officer's tent in the middle of upstate New York?"

"Upstate New York? I don't remember the area being called that, but of course I remember the day."

He would need some geography lessons soon, among other things. Much had changed in the world. The next evening we returned to Germany, back the way we came. We left the stolen car in the parking lot of the inn, but brought our friend with us. Thayer kept his promise to Ingrid, burying her, unmarked, next to the man she had loved.

Six Months Later

Mills and Jack were in France. I very much wanted to see my friend. I had been thinking of her a lot lately. Thayer and

I spent most of the last six months holed up in Berlin, reacquainting ourselves with each other. It was important to me for the people I loved most to also become acquainted, even friends.

The happy couple purchased a fixer-upper chateau on the outskirts of Annecy. The chateau was small as they went, around 5,000 square feet. I knew Mills was having as much fun remodeling her mini castle as she was living with Jack.

It was just past twilight when we pulled around the circular, graveled drive. Over the phone, she said the place was dilapidated. I couldn't for the life of me see what she meant. The exterior was gorgeous; creamy stone with modern windows, flanked by dark-gray shutters, all topped with a new slate roof. She must have already completed the outside work.

I stepped out of the car, looking around. I could see her in the landscaping, as well. Mills did not care for perfectly groomed hedges. She preferred them a touch wild, and she loved fragrant flowers. Blooms of red, purple, yellow, and orange danced around the edges of the beautiful home. The sound of running water reached my ears. There must be a good-size stream on the back of the property.

The door opened. Before I knew what was happening, Mills had me pinned to the side of the car. "Six months is unacceptable, Annie," she shouted in my ear.

"I know, I know," I said, laughing, trying not to choke on tendrils of blonde hair.

"Come in, I can't wait to show you everything." She turned toward Thayer. "Oh, hello. You must be him; the mysterious man inside the tent." She beamed, extending her hand. She looked lovely, happier than I'd ever seen her.

Thayer took it gently, placing his other hand over hers. "And you must be the fair aristocrat."

"Noble, dear," she said, winking.

Thayer laughed, bowing over her hand with an exaggerated flourish. I thought these two would get along.

We went inside where chaos reigned.

"The outside of this place is a lie," I said, taking it all in. Despite the wreck, I could see why she chose it. The home would be spectacular when she was finished.

Millicent laughed. "A horrible lie, but we'll get there. That's half the fun. We do have the important things; electricity, running water. The second floor is in better shape. I promise your room is quite nice."

Jack descended from the rickety staircase. "Well, hello, Annie." He looked much better than the last time I saw him. When I left Savannah, Jack was still mortal, recovering from the wounds inflicted by Alexandre. Now he looked the picture of health in jeans and a t-shirt; strong and glowing.

I hugged him, then introduced Thayer. I hoped they would find some things in common, as I wished to be alone with my friend for a bit. We had a hundred things to talk about. Mills read the look on my face.

She kissed Jack on the cheek, then said, "Why don't you take Thayer upstairs to their room?"

He kissed her back with a lingering look of love, not lost on anyone in the room.

She took my hand, leading me out the back of the chateau. I was correct about the water. There was a little stream, right where I thought it would be. But the star was the small lake, about twenty yards from the back door, off to one side of the property. We walked toward it, beckoned forth by the freshwater smells. How I loved this place already.

"So, how are you?" I started.

She looked away, fiddling her fingers together. "Oh, I'm wonderful. Jack is wonderful. This is the life I always wanted, you know?"

"Yes, but that isn't what I mean. How are you since Alexandre?" This was the first time I said his name out loud since that night. An involuntary shudder went through me.

Mills shrugged her shoulders as we continued to walk the perimeter of the lake. Every now and then, the sound of fish jumping in the water reached my ears. Further away, the rustling sounds of deer walking through the trees beyond could be heard. The sky was clear with stars shining bright and not a single cloud to darken our path. This was the kind of country life I had always longed for. "All right, I guess. Is it crazy that I feel relieved, but miss him and feel terribly guilty?"

"Of course, it isn't. I miss him, too. Parts of him, anyway. I realized long ago his disinterest in me. There was a reason why he waited to change you. He cared about you, wanted to make sure you were ready. With me, he just did it, not caring how it would turn out."

She reached for my hand, grasping it. "We have to move on. No more living in the old days. No more talk of Alexandre. I finally have a future I'm excited for. So, do you. That's what we should focus on. I'm tired of living in the blackness of the past."

I squeezed her hand. She was right. Mills knew too well what living in the past could do to a person. My future with Thayer was exciting. A real future, with nothing to fear; no obstacles to overcome. Settling in to a normal routine with him was as natural as a human taking a breath of air.

"How is Jack handling the whole undead thing?"

She groaned. "You know I hate the term *undead*. It makes us sound like re-animated corpses."

"Aren't we?" I couldn't help myself. I'd missed our banter.

"You may be, but I most certainly am not." She giggled. "Anyway, he's doing well. It's all been rather seamless. His change wasn't difficult, at all. And you know what's funny? He said he didn't experience the deepest midnight effect."

"I don't think it's funny. He knew wholeheartedly he wanted the change. It makes perfect sense. How about the whole researching what we are, where we come from thing? Have you found anything interesting?"

Millicent pulled a funny face. "Well, I haven't gotten to that, yet. I've been a little busy. But I will. Now, my turn for a question. Why did you never tell me about what Thayer meant to you? I can't believe you were able to keep something so meaningful from me."

"Honestly, Mills, you were so new in your grief back then. I didn't want to add to your troubles. I thought Thayer had moved on without me, so why rehash it, you know?"

"I did always wonder why you had such a thing for Germans. And, I'm sorry, Annie. I feel so awful for always putting the burden of my pain on everyone else. I know dealing with me wasn't easy."

I pulled her to a stop, taking both of her hands in mine. "It was no burden. Everyone grieves differently. I would have always been there for you, even if Jack had never happened."

We embraced, my eternal sister and I. "I love you so much, Annie. I hope you guys stay for a while."

"Ditto, babe. I think we will."

I felt like a solitary stroll. I left my three housemates engaged in a serious discussion about kitchen countertops to enjoy the cool, night air. The town was as quaint as any I had ever seen, with gentle rolling hills and small canals winding through the little city. I could see why it was called the "Venice of Savoie." I delighted in walking up and down the close, cobblestone streets, peeking into the shop windows. Exploring this city would be a joy.

About halfway through the small, provincial town, I stopped dead in my tracks. My eyes were playing tricks on me; too much drama lately. I closed my eyes, rubbing them for good measure. When I opened them again, he hadn't moved. But his face had changed. A wide, devilish grin broke out from ear to ear.

"Alexandre," I whispered.

A thrill of terror electrified my body, which remained rooted to its spot. Panic flooded my brain. I thought of those I loved, happily ensconced in Mills' dream home, talking shallowly of home improvements. If we hadn't destroyed him before, how would we do so now?

"It isn't possible," I hadn't meant to say this out loud, but I had.

"What the two of you know about our kind, I could fit in the palm of my hand," he said, pushing himself off the wall. He took a step toward me.

I backed up, my senses on high alert. He stopped, putting up his hands. "I won't hurt you, Annie." I thought of Mills. "I won't hurt her, either. I simply wanted to see you once more and ask you to give Millicent a message."

"Why?" I didn't trust this one bit.

"I'm not as crazy as all that, Annie. Really. I suppose I did lose it a little there, at the end." He paused. "But having your head lopped off, after a battle with your progeny. Well, that really makes you think." Here was Alexandre, after everything, standing in front of me, trying to be charming. I didn't take my eyes off him for a second.

"About that," I said, pointing to his head. I had to know.

He touched his neck. "The brain has to be destroyed, love. Fortunately, for me, the two of you made it rather easy by burying me with my head. So, thanks for the small favor." He grinned, again. His damn, charming, likable grin.

Of course, this was why Ingrid said we must destroy Emilia's brain and why Emilia had done the same to sweet Ingrid. I felt stupid. Alexandre hadn't occurred to me then. I suppose it made sense, in a twisted way. The cut flesh of an immortal would mend itself together in seconds. Decapitation was just another type of cut, albeit a more severe one. However, the same principles would apply. I imagined the mending process took some time.

"What now? You expect me to believe after all that, you can just leave her alone? Surely, there's a catch." I stood rigidly still, expecting him to attack me at any time.

"No catch, my dear. Tell her she's free. She doesn't have to fear me. There's nothing worse than loving someone who doesn't love you back, Annie. I really have come to my senses."

I didn't say anything. This seemed like another kind of madness. Emilia and Alexandre; was this what we all had to look forward to, if we lived long enough? Ingrid was right; we'd all go mad in the end. Something told me this wasn't the last I would see of my maker.

Alexandre simply smiled, inclined his head, and turned away. When he was almost to the end of the street, I called out, "Alexandre, I'm sorry."

He didn't turn around. He kept walking, raising his hand in farewell.

Book Three in the Immortal Kindred Series *available now!...*

HERE'S A SNEAK PEEK AT KING OF KINGS...
BOOK THREE IN THE IMMORTAL KINDRED SERIES.

The finely decorated lobby was full of posh men and women, all wearing their best designer clothes and bespoke suits. Bria wasn't fazed in the least by her surroundings as she devoured a granola bar, crumbs falling to the marble floor. She was wildly out of place here and I kind of loved it. Her flaming hair was enough to draw attention. Her clothing, which screamed survivalist, made her that much more conspicuous.

I moved up behind her. "You deserve a spanking for the ruckus in the hallway."

"The man who spanks me is suicidal," she said in a loud voice, drawing even more looks from the guests and staff.

Bria began walking toward the glittering revolving door, not bothering to see if I followed.

We took the train to the coast, making it just in time. Bria chided me the entire way for "sleeping in". I couldn't wait until we were on the boat with what I hoped was a roaring motor.

Available Now!

ABOUT THE AUTHOR

A.D. Brazeau is an award-winning author who writes what she loves. From dark and fantastical fairytale retellings to quirky romance, and everything in between, she loves nothing more than to immerse herself in new worlds. A.D. Brazeau is a book-obsessed wife, mother, and dog lover, who grew up surrounded by stories. Not much has changed. A.D. is from Colorado Springs, Co, and currently resides in Orange County, Ca.

BOOK ONE OF THE IMMORTAL KINDRED SERIES

True love never dies.

For Millicent, a once French noblewoman turned immortal vampire, forever is a long time to live in despair. The love of her life is murdered the night she becomes immortal. Millicent spends her endless night in a melancholy which never ends. Two hundred forty years later, she locks eyes with an English actor, who happens to look exactly like her long dead love.

Sadness turns to happiness as Millicent and Jack find passion in each other's arms. Their fling quickly turns serious as Millicent finds happiness once again—

and possibly her one true love.

However, their relationship becomes complicated by her own uncertainty, Jack's mortality, and the other man in Millicent's life, Alexandre, her maker and companion. When Alexandre puts his foot down, Millicent must decide if she's going to continue to be led by others or take the reins and drive the outcome of her life.

Deepest Midnight is set in modern day Savannah, Ga with occasional glimpses back to 18th century France. This is the first book in The Immortal Kindred Series.

Available at all major book retailers